SECRETS OF THE FALLS

THE LOOP BREAKER

BOOK TWO

RUSS THOMPSON

Books may be purchased by contacting the publisher and author at:

ISBN: 978-1-947782-21-1

Winterwolf Press

8635 West Sahara Ave. #425

Las Vegas, NV 89117

www.WinterwolfPress.com

Info@WinterwolfPress.com

Cover art by Laura C. Cantu

Interior design and formatting by Laura C. Cantu

Cover design © 2025 by Winterwolf Press

Cover art and Chapter art © 2025 by Winterwolf Press

I would like to dedicate this book to anyone who has ventured off course and come back to themselves and their true calling, and to anyone who has felt outcast, alone, or like they don't fit into the situation they find themselves in. I would like to thank my family and friends for their continued support and encouragement and to Christine Contini for inspiriting the main character, Lee Ann Daniels. I would also like to thank Laura Cantu for her vision and all of her hard work.

CONTENTS

CHAPTER
ONE

THROWING OFF AND MOVING FORWARD

L ee Ann draped her arms over the rusty gate at the front of her family's property on Green Creek Road and gazed out at the deep green foliage on either side of her and across the road. The trees were shriveled and drooping from the lack of rain, seeming to want the passage of the seasons or at least the relief of a brief rain shower that could break July's spell. Lee Ann felt a kinship with her anthropomorphized vision of the trees. She felt stuck in this place and was also ready for summer to end, ready to move on with the next phase of her life. Lee Ann took out her sketchpad and began to depict the trees and give them faces. After a few minutes, she turned the pages to look at her work from when she first came here-she fixated on a sketch she did of the creek on the day she first arrived at her father's place. She noticed how much more detail she was now adding to her sketches, how she had developed a much keener eye.

It was funny how benign and beautiful the woods were to Lee Ann in those days, considering the events that transpired in the nearby wildlife preserve almost two years ago. What Lee Ann feared now was not the mysterious nature of lost souls roaming the woods but the scorn of the locals and the antics of curiosity seekers who periodically tried to drive past the property and catch a shot of Lee Ann. A few times, they even tried to approach the house. Her father, Charles chased down two young men one night a year previously who even tried to enter an open window and enter the house. Charles fired a warning shot with his twelve gauge into the air. The men got away, but Charles was confident that they wouldn't try such a thing again.

The internet had also been abuzz about Lee Ann, with one paranormal site calling her the 'teen spirit guide of the south' and another that called her 'Lee Ann the teenage loop breaker.' They were all flattering titles, but Lee Ann did not welcome the attention and simply wanted to live a normal life. She had been contacted repeatedly by psychic societies, news outlets and vloggers who wanted permission to make Youtube documentaries about her and the legend of Thief's Hollow. She refused all of them and did her best to hide herself away from the world. The world however, kept wanting to know about her.

She allowed her hair to grow out and changed it back to its natural brown color. When she went to town, she tied her hair up in a ponytail, put on a cap and dark sunglasses like a teenaged Gretta Garbo. She would get what she needed and come directly back home, but people still recognized her despite her best efforts. Recently, Lee Ann noticed several ladies at the Save a Lot whispering amongst themselves as she walked by. Upon exiting the store, she heard a cat call from a group of young men who had spotted her from across the street. 'Hey witch girl. I got some pesky spirits at my house. Can you come get rid of them?' a tall lanky one shouted as his friends erupted with laughter. Lee Ann thought he looked like a clown with his large round curled mop with the cap sitting atop it, pencil thin mustache, awful posture and overly rosy cheeks that gave him the appearance of a drunk vulture.

"I can't help you with your spirits, but I could help you learn some respect for women," Lee Ann shot back as the drunk vulture's friends' jaws dropped open. She took off quickly down the street to avoid any reprisal. The incident left her feeling confident, bringing a smile to her face as she left the town behind in the lengthening afternoon shadows.

She sat cross-legged on the porch swing waiting for David to come and pick her up so that they could take an afternoon hike up to Widow's Bluff, a place they had bonded over when Lee Ann first moved to Laverne. David was the reason Lee Ann hadn't already left Laverne and the fact that she had to finish high school if any college was going to admit her.

David pulled up in his newly acquired '74 Mustang that he had worked years to save up for. Instead of smiling and making a joke like he used to, he rolled down the car window, gave Lee Ann a half-smile and spoke softly. The blue car glistened in the sun, its vibrance heightened by the recent waxing David had given it.

"Are you ready to go?" he asked solemnly, his long bangs hiding his glassy eyes.

"Are we going on a hike or to a funeral?" she answered as she climbed the green gate.

"Sorry, I guess the fact that you're leaving is hanging over everything," he said, cutting to the chase.

Lee Ann climbed in the car, put her sunglasses on and pulled her hoodie over her head and immediately turned to him, pulling his face towards hers. She kissed him quickly but lovingly and squeezed his hand.

"Don't worry, David. We are still together. I'm not leaving you; I'm leaving Laverne. Besides, Farthington is not my forever home and it's just two hours away. You can visit me anytime, and I can visit you."

"It's not quite the same," he replied as he pulled off onto the road, driving faster than normal as an expression of his agitation.

"Wow, easy there, Speed Racer," she said.

"What's Speed Racer?" David asked.

"You know, one of those vintage tv shows that I love," she responded.

David was quiet until they reached the trailhead for Widow's Bluff.

"I don't like this new quiet and brooding David," Lee Ann prodded. "Let's not let the rest of our time here together be like this."

"It's not that simple!" David closed the car door with a bit more force than he normally would have and took off down the trail.

"Wait up, Charlie Brown," she joked as she ran after him and pushed him gently to get his attention.

"Stop!" he protested.

"David, have you not listened to anything I've said?"

"I did, but like I said, it's not that easy for me. I'm left here with nothing but a mechanic's apprenticeship with my uncle. There are no college opportunities for me," he lamented.

"There is no shame in a career like that, and you could do it anywhere. Besides, you still can finish your diploma at the adult education classes in town." David grimaced at the thought of going back to school and answered Lee Ann with complete silence. David's lack of interest or achievement in academics was a topic that Lee Ann rarely broached with him, although it secretly concerned her. She knew that he was extremely intelligent and good at solving hands-on problems. He just didn't have the knack for school. He would easily become fidgety, bored, and distracted and his parents never got him tested to see if he might have some learning disability. Otherwise, he might have received medication or assistance that could have helped him focus.

Finally, the trail opened to a rocky outcrop and an expansive view just beyond it. Lee Ann squeezed David's hand, turned to him, and smiled.

"You see that view? The way the river valley just opens up, and the rushing waters turn the corner and flow on to parts unknown? That's your life and its possibilities," She offered.

David smiled, but it turned into a giggle. "You sound like our old guidance counselor, Mr. Gibbons," he snickered.

"I'm serious, David. You can do whatever you want and be whatever you want. There are other avenues for you besides college. You have all kinds of skills that I don't. You have... how can I say this... an intuitive gift with your hands."

"Now you sound like Katrina," David said, pointing to their friend's verbose nature.

"It's true, though David. You are what is holding you back. I learned that lesson the hard way out in those woods," Lee Ann insisted.

"Let's psychoanalyze me later," he said, looking away from her towards the view.

"I'm sorry David. I just want what's best for you... for us," she said, putting her arms around him.

"I know," he said as he turned towards her, smiled, and hugged her tightly as the sun began to spread out its myriad colors across the horizon. The view at Widow's Bluff was wide and expansive, offering a sweeping view of the river to the west and the forested slopes to the east that included Lee Ann's place and the land beyond it. As they turned away from each other towards the view, they noticed some smoke rising in a small plume towards the direction of Lee Ann's property.

Lee Ann and David looked at each other for a moment, thinking the same thing.

"That's too close for comfort, that looks like the woods over by your place. Let's check it out!" David said as they turned to run down the trail back towards the car.

First, they pulled up to Lee Ann's place. They got out and saw smoke billowing upwards, behind their property in the all too familiar direction of the wildlife preserve and thief's hollow. It seemed to have grown since they spotted it atop Widow's Bluff.

"It's at the hollow, c'mon!" David shouted, pulling Lee Ann by the hand. Charles and Shirley saw them through the kitchen window, running through the yard, towards the garden and the woods beyond.

"What's going on?" Shirley asked no one in particular.

"I'm going to find out," Charles answered, and proceeded to run after Lee Ann and David. He caught up to them at the edge of the woods.

"Everything alright, punkin?" Charles inquired.

"We don't know, there's smoke rising up from the area around the hollow," Lee Ann answered between breaths as they crossed the creek and headed deeper into the woods. With each step, Lee Ann had flashes of memories as the smell of the fire grew in its intensity. When she closed her eyes for a moment, she could see the cabin burning again and the children running for their lives. Despite how real the visions seemed, she knew that they had no sway over her, and she continued forward without fear. What gave her pause was why these events were being presented to her again. It made her wonder for a moment if all the souls trapped in the area had in fact crossed over like she thought they had two years previously.

"I'll go and grab the fire extinguisher in the kitchen," Charles stated and turned to head back to the house.

Lee Ann and David continued through the woods, making their way past the boundary of the wildlife preserve. When Lee Ann and David made it to the ridge above the fabled hollow, the smell of burning wood permeated their nostrils. Charles caught up to them a moment later, clutching the fire extinguisher. He was out of breath after carrying it up the steep slope.

"Why is this happening again?" Lee Ann muttered fretfully, gripping David's hand.

"I don't know," he answered helplessly, pulling her into his arms.

Charles headed down the slope into the hollow. He had a curious but skeptical glint in his eye.

"It's nothing supernatural at all. Just a campfire gotten out of hand." He reasoned.

When he reached the bottom of the slope, Charles saw a small clearing to his left where a campfire was ablaze and had set fire to the leafy ground adjacent to it. The flames were spreading fast towards the forest edge. The smoke was thick and intense. Charles coughed as he began to put the flames out with the extinguisher.

Lee Ann and David ran over towards Charles and began to help him, stomping on the small flames where the fire had begun to spread.

Lee Ann and Charles took out their water bottles that they had with them for their hike and did their best to douse the flames with the water.

"I'll run back to the creek and get more!" David declared. He ran back up the slope carrying the two water bottles while Lee Ann and Charles continued to extinguish the flames. David returned a few minutes later, helping to put out the remaining embers.

"Whew!" Charles said, "A few minutes more and those woods would have been ablaze. That could have taken out the entire wildlife preserve."

Lee Ann was speechless, but relieved. She noticed something glinting in the afternoon sunlight over by the site of the campfire. She went over and picked up a cell phone that had been dropped in the leaves. Although it was locked, there was a screenshot of three twenty-something guys standing together with the initials, 'P. I. S' above their heads. Under their picture, the meaning of the letters was revealed: Paranormal Investigation Squad.

Lee Ann chuckled and took the phone over to where Charles and David were standing.

"You see, this is why I have to get out of here," she stated.

"These damn curiosity seekers won't rest until they destroy this place," Charles opined.

CHAPTER
TWO
TUG OF WAR

"What happened?" Shirley inquired.

"Damn campfire got out of control over in the preserve," Charles shared.

"Yeah, I thought things were starting up all over again for a minute there," Lee Ann added.

"Dear lord, should we call the sheriff or the ranger?" Shirley asked.

"I suppose the ranger 'cuz the fire was in the wildlife preserve–Thief's Hollow, more specifically. We have their cell phone, so there can be little doubt who they were," Charles said.

"Of course, it had to be Thief's Hollow. Oh, Lee Ann I am so sorry you had to go through that. I'm sure it was triggering," Shirley said, patting Lee Ann's back. This show of empathy and affection had grown between them over the last couple of years, and Lee Ann really liked how it felt.

"Thanks, Shirl, but to tell the truth I was only afraid that the forest was going to catch on fire. I knew deep down inside that there wasn't really anything to fear," she said, giving her a full hug.

Charles went into the next room to call the ranger. Lee Ann washed her hands to help Shirley prepare dinner for that night. They were going to have all of Lee Ann's friends over to celebrate Lee Ann's acceptance at Farthington College and to say goodbye. Lee Ann was silent and reflective as she took a baking dish out of the cabinet.

"You ok?" Shirley asked her.

"Not really, to be honest. I mean, don't get me wrong I know going off to school is the right thing to do. I just don't know why it is for me, specifically," she said, causing Shirley to scrunch up her face in confusion.

"What do you mean?" Shirley inquired.

"What I mean is that I don't know what I want to study there. I know I've told you this before, but it doesn't ever really go away. All I know right now is that I want to use my talents and passions to drive what I do whether that's my career or whatever I decide to do."

"Everyone feels a bit like that when they get out of high school, honey. It can be overwhelming being expected to know what you want to do with the rest of your life when you're eighteen years of age," Shirley admitted.

"Did you feel like that too?" Lee Ann asked, leaning in slightly.

"Of course! But you shouldn't use my shoddy example. I ended up getting pregnant and dropping out, but hey, life happens," Shirley admitted with a smile.

"You're not a shoddy example," Lee Ann said. "I just wish that dad would consider letting me go to the art college like I want to. Especially since they are willing to give me a partial scholarship!"

"You know how he feels about that. He's afraid that you will end up without a way to make a living for yourself, and the Francis College of Art is so far away. A nine-hour drive is almost too far to come home for the weekend," Shirley reasoned.

Charles came downstairs and smiled at the two of them.

"Everything alright?" he asked.

"Sure, everything's fine. We were just commiserating about the uncertainty that comes with starting college and figuring out what to do with your life," Shirley revealed.

"Well, I'm sure that will come to you. The important thing is that Lee Ann is takin' the next responsible step in her life. Besides, ain't there basic courses everyone must take regardless of what their major is?"

"It's weird when you talk about me like I'm not in the room, dad, but yes that's true," Lee Ann remarked. "The thing is, you know I know what I want to be and where I wanted to go to school." A hint of hostility snuck into her tone.

"We've been over this so many times, the important thing is that YOU are pursuing your higher education and working on a degree that you can one day use. I wish I had."

"You turned out alright, didn't you?" Lee Ann laughed.

"That's debatable," Shirley said making Charles scrunch up his face. Shirley and Lee Ann looked at each other and laughed again.

Soon, Lee Ann's friends began to arrive at the house. She felt happy to see them, but her feelings were tinged with a hint of sadness knowing that she would soon have to say her goodbyes. Katrina was the first to arrive, followed by David, then Jasmine, and finally, Felicity. Lee Ann was unable to hold back a tear as she hugged each one of them. David sat down beside Lee Ann at the dinner table across from Katrina and Jasmine. Felicity sat on the other side of Lee Ann. Charles sat down beside Felicity, and a space was left on his right for Shirley who was still preparing the last of the dinner in the kitchen.

Lee Ann looked around at all her friends, trying to take in their appearances and cherish them for posterity: Katrina smiled back, pushing up her full rosy cheeks flanked by her bob-style haircut. She wore a red t-shirt and an unbuttoned red and black checkered flannel. Ever since Lee Ann met Katrina, she had worn some combination of red and black. She would miss Katrina's enthusiasm and her verbose take on any topic that might come up in conversation.

Jasmine smiled beneath her purple headband that kept her hair tied up. She wore a long, matching purple dress. Recently, she had dreaded her hair; Lee Ann thought about how good it looked on her and how much she would miss her soft-spoken words of wisdom and kindness. Lee Ann's gaze shifted over to David who was looking at her curiously through the bangs that hung in his eyes.

"You ok?" he whispered as Jasmine and Katrina began to chat.

"Yeah, I'll be fine. I'm just not good at long goodbyes," she whispered back as she gripped his hand underneath the table. Felicity smiled at Lee Ann in that moment, prompting Lee Ann to smile back. Felicity had one of her typical floral-print dresses on with a blue and silver shawl around her neck. The large bangles she wore in her ears made her look the fortune teller part.

Lee Ann sensed a telepathic message being exchanged.

You are going to be ok, Felicity seemed to say to her.

I hope so she answered back, not feeling at all that she would be, being apart from David and her friends for so long.

"Hello everyone and welcome!" Shirley said as she entered the dining room carrying dishes of food.

"Let us help you!" Katrina said, getting out of her chair.

"Nonsense, hun. I got this. You just stay there and visit," Shirley insisted as she turned to grab more dishes. She had prepared Lee Ann's favorite dish, vegetarian lasagna, along with garlic bread and a giant salad bowl brimming with lettuce, tomatoes, and cucumbers.

"Wow, this looks delectable, Mrs. Daniels," Katrina remarked.

"Thanks hun, it's the least I could do," Shirley said, finally sitting down at the table herself.

"I just want to start by saying how lucky Lee Ann truly is to have such great friends," Charles said as he raised his beer to them and took a swig.

"Thank you," they all said, practically in unison.

"I'm not great at saying eloquent things at moments like this, but I want everyone to know how much I love and appreciate you. I never would have been able to make it through what happened two years ago without all of you. I mean it." Lee Ann did her best to be stoic and fight off her tears as David squeezed her hand tighter under the table.

"You have always had the strength you needed. You just needed that support to see that," Felicity offered. Jasmine and Katrina nodded their head in agreement.

"So, do you know what your major is going to be yet?" Katrina asked Lee Ann.

"Well, I'm not entirely sure yet. As long as I can remember the only thing I wanted to do is to become an artist. So, maybe art history?" she answered. Charles shot Shirley an uncertain glance.

"You have plenty of time to figure that out as you take your required courses, but just make sure you study somethin' you can use when you get out 'hun," Charles added.

"An art history major could land you a good teaching job," Katrina said, rushing to Lee Ann's defense.

"Yeah, you can get a teaching job anywhere," Jasmine added.

"Look to where your passions lie, give it time to unfold and speak to you," Felicity allowed. Her kind smile and calm demeanor comforted Lee Ann. She knew Felicity was right. It was ok for her to feel uncertain at age eighteen about the course of her future; she had time for her life path to present itself.

"You can do that while you're working on the requirements," Charles quickly inserted.

Lee Ann shot him a quick glare and then looked away.

After dinner, the table was lively with conversation as the four friends reminisced about their high school days. They recalled the time Lee Ann stood up to Mary Hartford when she tried to bully Katrina.

"She really had it coming. I wonder what mean girl squad she'll be a part of in college?" Katrina commented as Jasmine and Lee Ann laughed in response.

As the hour grew late, their conversation shifted towards the events surrounding Thief's Hollow, an experience that would forever unite them.

"Do you really think that the curse has been lifted from the place once and for all?" Jasmine mused.

"Yes, but it wasn't a curse. It was simply the imprint of events that happened long ago, like a footprint that is preserved in just the right sediment. With Lee Ann's help, the imprint has now been removed, and the souls who were lost have now found their way," Felicity shared.

Lee Ann felt like this was the perfect moment to share something with all her friends that she had been working on. Only her parents and David had seen it so far, and she was anxious for Jasmine, Felicity, and Katrina to see how she had spent much of the summer. She stood up and clanged a spoon on her water glass.

"Now I would like for you guys to see what I've been working on for several months now. Follow me," she said as she began to walk towards the spare room down the hallway. Katrina and Jasmine shared a look of wonderment about what it could be. When the group entered the spare room, they saw several canvases leaning against the wall. Two of the largest ones were propped up on easels. Each picture depicted some aspect of the events at Thief's Hollow all in Lee Ann's unique impressionism meets expressionistic style. Her chosen medium was oil paints; she liked the way that she could apply thick layers of coloration to the canvas. The largest painting showed Lee Ann gazing at a spectral figure emerging from the woods with colorful blue orbs in the tree behind it. Another showed the ominous Klan members making their way through the woods.

"These are amazing! Oh my god, it's like Monet and Munch got together and collaborated on these. I've never seen such vibrant color and emotion depicted on canvas!" Katrina swooned. David rolled his eyes at Katrina's references, which he didn't much understand. He had seen the paintings several times, so they didn't have the same effect on him.

"Lee Ann, you have captured the essence of these events

perfectly, down to the emotional impact," Felicity said as she put a hand on Lee Ann's shoulder.

"They are incredible! You are a master!" Jasmine added.

"Thank you, everyone. I feel pretty good about them," Lee Ann said.

"You should be very proud," Felicity stated, feeling that Lee Ann was shortchanging herself.

The evening grew late, and everyone began to depart. Felicity was the last to leave and she continued to talk to Lee Ann after her parents went inside the house.

"I wanted to wait until I had you alone to talk with you." She spoke softly as if she were afraid someone might overhear.

"Ok, I'm all ears," Lee Ann responded.

"I just simply wanted to remind you not to forget your gifts. Your abilities as an artist are outstanding, and I sense that you are trying to downplay that or don't fully realize the scope of your talents." Felicity's forehead was creased with concern, but the kindness in her smile made Lee Ann feel reassured.

"I know, I just felt the need to express something after all that's happened. I know I have a long way to go to be as good as I want to be though..."

"You are farther along than you think you are. You need to give yourself credit for what you've accomplished and not just with your painting." Lee Ann's face revealed her doubts.

"Well, that gift is something that I hope I don't ever have to use again. Looking back, it was so stressful."

Felicity's smile ran away from her face.

"Lee Ann, do not forget how truly special you are. Do not forget how the whole experience we went through helped you to get a handle on your grief and the fear that threatened to consume you. Your special gifts will guide you towards your truth. Also remember that other peoples' opinions about you and your future choices are like shadows that we are trying to interpret, like Plato's allegory of the cave. We cannot fully realize ourselves through other people's lenses; we must fill in the colorful details for ourselves to truly see our true selves. In the end, only you can know what the best choices are for you, and you will make them." Felicity's smile returned to her face as she grasped both of Lee Ann's hands. Although she knew Felicity was right, it was hard for her to feel complete confidence in herself. However, she did take comfort in Felicity's confidence in her as she hugged her goodbye in the driveway under a moonlit sky.

CHAPTER
THREE
NEW BEGINNINGS

Saying goodbye to David was much harder for Lee Ann than she thought it would be. He began crying before she did, which she did not expect, and it was impossible for her to hold back the tears once he started.

"You can come visit me really soon!" she reassured him as she pulled away to look him in the eyes.

"I.... I know," he said, wiping his nose on his sleeve. He took a deep breath and smiled at her, trying to compose himself.

Charles was waiting in the truck.

"You'd better get going," David said. Lee Ann kissed him once more and squeezed his hand.

"I'm always with you," She reassured him, flashing back to the time when her mother uttered the same words that gave her so much comfort.

"I know," David answered, feeling a bit like Han Solo when Leia said she loved him.

"I love you!" David surprised himself as if someone else was speaking through him, but he knew it was his feelings pouring forth unhindered by any inhibitions.

"I love you too, David!" She answered. As difficult as it was, she finally pulled away and got in the truck, not looking back for fear that she would completely lose it if she had to see David's morose expression.

"You alright, punkin?" Charles asked. By now Lee Ann had given up telling her father not to call her that. By this time, she had come to expect it, but it never failed to annoy her.

She said very little to her father on the way to the college as the bustle of the occasional town gave way to the far more common woods, fields, and hills of the passing landscape. The hills seemed to climb higher the further east they went. Lee Ann put on her head-phones, closed her eyes, and tried to drift off to someplace else where she didn't have to feel the loss of leaving her old life behind. She wanted to float far away from her father and leave him alone to drive away and out of her sight. It was an odd feeling that she hadn't expected having been so excited about going off to school up to now.

"Sure is pretty, the drive that is," Charles remarked, trying to start a conversation with the daughter that he would soon miss sorely. She acted like she didn't hear and continued trying to fall asleep. As she closed her eyes, she felt as if she was being forced into a corner like a child who is put in time out. She felt that she had no recourse but to sit there and allow herself to be carted away to Farthington.

I should be headed to the art college, Lee Ann tried to push the thought away as soon as it surfaced, but she could not help but feel the sting of regret for not fighting her father more on this coupled with bitterness.

Why doesn't he ever listen to me?

Charles found a station that played classic country artists like Loretta Lynn and Hank Williams and tried to clear his mind. Despite his resolve, he did feel a pang of guilt for forcing his will on his daughter. Every time these thoughts infringed on his consciousness, he fought back by reassuring himself that Lee Ann had to be directed towards a career and that being an artist wasn't a real career unless you were incredibly lucky enough to become famous.

They reached the gates of Farthington and stared at its gothic-like architecture together in silence. It looked rather out of place the way it was placed in the middle of nowhere in its sprawled-out grandeur. Tall, collegiate buildings with sharp, pointed arches rose up out of the trees on either side of them, clothed in rose marble that had been mined from nearby sources. They gazed out with large windows that illuminated its large, buttressed hallways within. A security booth lay just ahead in front of an elaborate twelve-foot-tall rod iron gate. Beyond the gate was the main business offices in a simple, rectangular building. Just behind the business office was the main hall and a clock tower that was also the school library. The lecture halls and departments were laid out in a quad perpendicular to the clock tower. At the very back of the campus, at the edge of a wild tract of land, were the dorms laid out like large cabins at a summer camp.

The guard peered at Charles as if he'd taken a wrong turn to have ended up there.

"Name please?" the guard asked before Charles could get a word out.

"Charles Daniels. I'm here to drop off my daughter, Lee Ann Daniels," he said with a friendly grin that the guard did not return. He looked through some paperwork and at a laptop computer and finally spoke,

"Straight down the main road to the main hall. Your mentor will meet you there. Welcome to Farthington!" With that he finally managed to give Lee Ann a small grin which she returned.

They pulled up to the main student hall with its large triangular shape and sturdy wooden doors. A well dressed girl in a white blouse and brown skirt drove up in a golf cart. She had medium-length, dark brown hair that was tied back and a perky smile that hid her narrow dark eyes.

"You must be Lee Ann," she said as they got out of the truck.

"I am," she said, still in a bit of shock at her new surroundings.

"Wow, that's some nice architecture," Charles stated, trying not to seem like a country bumpkin. He proceeded to get Lee Ann's luggage out of the back seat.

"It's nice to meet you. Welcome to Farthington. I'm your mentor, Julie!" she was louder and peppier this time.

"Thank you," Lee Ann answered simply.

"Here, let me help you with those," Julie said as she picked up one of Lee Ann's bags and began to load it into the golf cart.

"I got it, hun," Charles said, quickly scooping up the other bags that he quickly slipped onto the back of the cart.

"Well, I guess I will leave you to it then. I'll call you later and see how you're settling in," Charles said, putting a hand on his daughter's shoulder. She stared back at him and put one of her hands on his shoulder as if to mock the gesture.

"Well, alrighty then, dad," she said.

Charles snuck in a quick hug, which Lee Ann somewhat reluctantly reciprocated.

"Bye now, take care of my Lee Ann," he said, waving to them as he drove away.

"So, are you ready to see the campus?" Julie asked.

"Sure," Lee Ann said, trying to make the best of things. The truth was. she was enamored with the architecture and the grounds. There seemed to be so many possibilities for artistic subjects all around her.

"When was this place founded?" Lee Ann asked.

"1847," Julie answered promptly.

"It was founded by Edward Goodwin Hurst, a philanthropist who wanted to create a collegial experience without the distractions of the city, surrounded by natural beauty."

"Wow, they need to put you in the marketing department," Lee Ann remarked, prompting another eyeless smile from Julie.

"Thank you."

"So, about that natural beauty. Are there like trails and such around?" Lee Ann inquired.

"Yes, there are several! We back up to part of the Southern Overlands Natural Area and there are waterfalls, views, you name it! As a matter of fact, the trail to Whispering Falls is not far from your dorm," Julie said as she stepped on the gas and drove the golf cart past the business office and down one of the four branches of the quad that spread out from the clock tower/library.

"Does this tour include those places?" Lee Ann continued.

"Haha, no, but I can show you where some of the closer ones are," Julie answered.

Lee Ann liked Julie although she didn't seem like the kind of person she'd normally hang out with- she seemed primmer and more proper than her usual friends. She tried to push the notion of what her friends should be like out of her mind.

Don't be a reverse snob!

"These are the Science and Mathematics departments here, Whetting Hall and Johnson Hall," Julie said motioning up towards the large triangular buildings that frowned down on them with their large windows and enormous wooden doors that all the buildings seemed to have. Lee Ann could vaguely see desks and chairs on the third and fourth floors.

"Where is the art department?" Lee Ann blurted out.

"Ah, well what we have is very small, but it is next to the History building, Gates Hall. We are going that way now. She pulled through a side road onto another branch of the quad. There were no people around because the quarter had ended and the next one would not start for another week. Lee Ann thought the buildings looked magnificent and dignified plopped down in the middle of the forest as if they were the relic of some forgotten civilization. She imagined the oral traditions they could pass on if the bricks could speak and say what they'd witnessed.

"There it is," Julie said as they rode past a modest, white house that stood next to another of the same tall, triangular buildings.

"Do they actually have classes in there?" Lee Ann asked, unable to hide how underwhelmed she was.

"Yes, they have a studio there," Julie reassured her. "We aren't generally known for our arts department, but we hope to grow it."

Lee Ann frowned a little as they continued their tour.

Finally, they made it through all the branches of the quad and headed towards the edge of the campus where the dormitories lay hidden in the trees.

Lee Ann was even more intrigued as the way narrowed, and the trees began to close in on either side.

"So, I get to stay back here?" Lee Ann's tone was changed now, slightly excited.

"Yes, all the dorms are back here. It's very scenic," she said.

"Where is yours?" Lee Ann asked.

"Oh, mine is over that way on what is called the west way." She pointed over towards the west and continued onwards. They passed two different cabin-like dwellings that looked somewhat like the cabins that the CCC built back in the thirties but were larger and fancier. It was rustic, more like a summer camp than a college dorm. Lee Ann was intrigued, leaning forward to soak in as much detail as she could.

"Here we are," Julie said as she pulled up to what looked to be the last cabin on the route. It looked lonely and dejected due to its position in the back with the dark cloak of the forest spread out just behind it and hills rising just beyond.

"Whoa, so I get the one right next to the woods? Awesome!" Lee Ann exclaimed, momentarily forgetting her disappointment at having to be at Farthington in the first place.

"Will I have a roommate? I did request having my own place, if possible," Lee Ann pointed out.

"As of now, you are by yourself, but our numbers are up so no guarantees that it will stay that way," Julie explained as she got out of the golf cart and walked up to the cabin. Lee Ann followed right behind her, studying the cabin. The outside was made from flattened rocks arranged in alternating patterns that gave it a stoic, strong quality. Its door and window frames were wooden. In the back, Lee Ann could just make out a screened porch facing out towards the woods. She smiled immediately realizing where she would spend most of her time while she was here. For the moment the roiling boil that had dominated her feelings was easing and cooling.

Julie unlocked the large, squeaky screen door and the thick oak door behind it. The door opened into a large room with bunk beds on either side. Large windows were positioned just above the top bunks. There was a large farm table with chipping paint in the center of the room with four wooden chairs around it. A vase full of daisies had been placed in the center, giving it a homely quality. In the back was a small kitchen with all the amenities and a door to the left led to the bathroom. Lee Ann thought about how much she wanted to remain alone with the lack of privacy the accommodations offered. She didn't much like how the beds were all together in a common space without the privacy that separate rooms afforded.

"So, you can choose whichever bed you like seeing as how you are on your own for now," Julie said with a smile.

"Thanks Julie, you really have been a big help."

"It's nothing but thank you!" Julie said with another huge smile.

"We should do something some time, hang out or something," Lee Ann suggested. Although she knew Julie had probably given a million tours like this and was probably just as nice to everyone else, she gave the tour to, Lee Ann could still sense that Julie was kind and genuine. Her sense of people's character was usually pretty accurate.

"Sure, that'd be great!" Julie agreed. "Well, for now, I will let you settle in. Dinner is at six, so I'll check in with you then. The mess hall as we all call it is just up the road back where we came in."

"I remember, thanks!" Lee Ann said returning Julie's smile. "I really appreciate it, Julie."

"Don't mention it. I'll see you tonight!" Julie said. Lee Ann watched her leave and drive away in the golf cart. Suddenly she felt very alone, but she was enamored with her surroundings. She went and sat on a rocker inside of the screened in porch and listened to the wind shake the leaves of the forest. Yawning, she took out her phone and saw five messages from David. She quickly answered him and closed her eyes, allowing herself to slip into a deep sleep.

CHAPTER

FOUR

UNEXPECTED COMPANY

When Lee Ann awoke, crickets were chirping all around her and the late afternoon sun had given way to a veil of stars and a crescent moon that lit up sky offering a sharp contrast to the dark line of trees in front of her. She looked at her phone and saw that she had been asleep for three hours and had missed dinner. Then she remembered the sandwiches that Shirley had packed for her. She took one of them out of her backpack and took a bite as she began to read the myriad texts David had sent her until he finally gave up. She was slightly annoyed at having to text so much despite how much she missed him. A part of her wanted to surrender to this new existence and just take it in without the distractions of the life she had left behind, if only temporarily. Then, she heard a noise coming from inside. She froze for a moment, contemplating its source. Was it Julie coming to see why she didn't show for dinner? Or was it an animal?

Lee Ann cautiously got up and opened the screen door that led to the main part of the cabin. It was dark inside and there was no sign of anyone. Lee Ann switched on the light and began to walk towards the kitchen.

"Hello!" a voice called out from the top bunk on Lee Ann's right. She turned quickly towards the sound of the voice and saw a girl sitting with her legs dangling over the side. Her face was half-hidden by the shadows, but Lee Ann could see that she had short bangs and a bob haircut. She wore a black t-shirt and grey shorts.

"Holy crap! You scared the beejesus out of me," Lee Ann responded.

"I am so sorry!" the girl said as she jumped down from the bunk onto the floor. Lee Ann could see that the girl was skinnier and shorter than she was. Her face was round, and her eyes were large and hazel green. She wore a t-shirt which bore the album cover of the first album by the Damned. She had a distant sadness about her that Lee Ann could identify with. She also had of bit of an edge about her, a hesitancy that Lee Ann couldn't quite put her finger on.

"Hey, I'm Connor," the girl said in a shy, soft voice. It seemed far off, like the voice of someone calling back to someone from a distance.

"I'm Lee Ann," She answered, trying to hide her disappointment at the presence at what looked to be her roommate.

"So, I guess we're roommates," Lee Ann spoke out to break the awkward silence.

"Yes," Connor said with a smile that suddenly disappeared. "I saw that you chose one of the bottom bunks, so I chose the upper bunk opposite you to give you space."

"I appreciate that. To tell the truth, I was hoping that I wouldn't have a roommate, no offense," Lee Ann divulged.

"That's ok, I'm an introvert. I won't get in your way," Connor insisted.

"No worries! I hope I didn't seem rude when I said I wanted to be alone, and you really seem cool. I really like your t-shirt. I like the Damned a lot, especially Machine Gun Etiquette," Lee Ann allowed.

"Thanks," Connor said as she lifted her head and seemed to become more comfortable in her surroundings.

"Why'd you come to Farthington?" Connor asked.

"Believe me, I ask myself that question a lot. Mainly, to study Art History and get as many actual studio classes in as I can," Lee Ann revealed.

"Yeah, you don't seem like the others," Connor commented.

"I haven't even met any of the others, other than Julie, my mentor. She was super nice. Otherwise, it's been kind of a ghost town around here." Connor gave her an odd look for a moment before responding.

"Well, by the time I got here, several others were starting to arrive. They were so, how do I say it, stuffy? Most of them just kind of looked at me if I tried to say hi."

"I figured it might be like that. I'm only here because of a scholarship. Otherwise, it would be far too rich for my blood."

"Same here. I'm here on an English scholarship," Connor shared.

"Ahh, well us two fish out of water will at least have each other then," Lee Ann said, feeling increasingly comforted by Connor's presence. She realized that if she had to have a roommate, Connor would be the perfect companion.

"I like that," Connor seemed to open up the more they talked. "Hey, want to go for a stroll?" she suggested, suddenly.

"At night? Where to?"

"There's a waterfall trail not too far from here and I'm feeling a bit restless," Connor revealed.

"Is it safe? I don't want to go tumbling down some ravine the first night I'm here," Lee Ann laughed.

"Oh, no, it's safe. There's a trail that climbs to the top of the falls, but we won't try to go there at night," Connor shared.

"How do you know so much about the trails around here?" Lee Ann inquired.

"I visited when I was looking around for schools to go to. The trails were one of the big things that decided it for me. C'mon, I'll show you." With a burst of energy, Connor moved quickly towards the door. Lee Ann followed, although she was still a bit reluctant for a night hike in an unfamiliar place.

The moon went behind the clouds, darkening the proceedings. Connor moved quickly and confidently along the edge of the forest to the east as the light outside of their cabin dissipated. After a couple hundred yards, a small, gravel road appeared to their right, parallel to them. Lee Ann wandered where it led to.

"That's the road you can take if you want to access the trailhead by car," Connor instructed as if she sensed Lee Ann's thoughts. Again, Lee Ann was impressed with Connor's knowledge of the place for someone who had only visited it once before.

The road turned towards them to intersect with a tiny parking lot with about four empty parking spaces and a trailhead just beyond with a small sign that read, 'Whispering Falls: 2.5- mile round-trip loop.' It was then that Lee Ann could hear the whisper of a stream moving through the night forest, just a few yards away from the trailhead.

"C'mon, this way!" Connor shouted, electing to take the left side of the loop. The trail was narrow and followed the small, rushing creek to their right. Lee Ann felt unsettled as she followed Connor down the trail. She took out her phone and turned on her flashlight to light her way. Connor didn't seem to have any need for such conveniences; she was moving quickly and confidently even though the moon was hiding behind the clouds, not allowing any light to illuminate their way. Lee Ann could smell the lush dampness of the forest mixed with cedar. It refreshed her and made her long to see the place in the daylight.

"We'll have to come back here during the day," Lee Ann suggested.

"Sure, I just couldn't wait to share this," Connor answered without looking back. The trail began a steady descent following a series of switchbacks until they were deep inside a circular cove lined with sharp, mossy ridges of limestone that sat like shelves dripping into the darkness around them. The trail soon hugged the rocky outcrops on the left with the forest dominating the right. The sound of rushing water became louder and more prominent the deeper they descended into the cove. The smell of evergreens and damp earth now permeated and echoed through the grotto. Lee Ann took a deep breath.

"Ahh, that smell! There's nothing like it!" her voice echoed as they moved towards the sound of falling water.

"Yes, I agree!"

They turned a sharp corner and could now clearly hear water breaking on the rocks repeatedly. Lee Ann looked up and could see the glint of the waterfall reflecting light from the moon that decided to make an appearance behind the curtain of clouds.

"Wow!" Lee Ann said as they moved closer to the falls. Lee Ann estimated it to be over a hundred feet high. The moon lit up the water as it dropped down a small cascade and over the main drop into a large pool below. The trail branched off to the right, towards the pool in one direction but continued underneath the falls if you maintained a forward trajectory. Connor took the right spur towards the pool. They stood in front of the falls, listening to its mesmerizing dance of water over the rocks and into the shimmering pool.

"Man, I wish I had my sketchbook. I will have to come back in the daylight!" Lee Ann mused. The place had captivated her enough for her to forget how much she hadn't wanted to come to this place. It rekindled her love for nature and bound her to it.

"C'mon, let's walk behind the falls!" Connor suggested.

"Cool!" Lee Ann followed Connor eagerly. When they got behind the falls, they could feel the cool spray of the water on their faces and see the moonlight reflected above them through the falling water.

"It's magical!" Lee Ann said, staring out into darkness the forest exuded beyond the light-reflecting waters. Her hands began to tingle, a familiar sensation that alarmed her. She looked all around her searching for a possible presence that could explain this.

"You ok?" Connor asked, turning to face her.

Then, something moved past Lee Ann's field of vision. It was the falling silhouette of a person, although she couldn't see where it fell, nor did she hear the splash of a body falling into the pool.

"Did you see that?" Lee Ann exclaimed.

"See what?" Connor inquired.

Lee Ann ran back around to the spur trail which led to the pool. She looked all around the pool and the edges as Connor came running after her.

"What did you see?" Connor asked.

"A body. Someone jumped from the top of the falls, I swear it!" Lee Ann stammered.

"Well, there's no one here now..." Connor hesitated.

Lee Ann took a deep breath and looked into Connor's sympathetic eyes.

"Are you alright?" Connor asked, putting her hand on Lee Ann's shoulder.

"I just need to get back," Lee Ann responded as she felt her breath steadily increasing.

CHAPTER

FIVE

LIKE A SORE THUMB

L ee Ann walked out of the cabin to take a stroll in the cool of the evening. She walked down one of the pebble-lined paths that led away from the cabins towards the lecture halls. For some strange reason, she was overwhelmed by the sensation that someone was behind her, but she was too unsettled to turn around and see who it might be. She broke into a jog trying to put some distance between herself and whatever might be behind her. Then she heard the voices- angry voices of a group of girls following her.

What do they want? She asked as she looked towards the sky as if it might answer her.

"Don't let her get away!" one of the voices cried out, prompting Lee Ann to break into a run.

Although she could have sworn that she was still on the pebble-lined pathway, she looked from side to side and realized that somehow the forest had closed in around her where before the surroundings were open and grassy.

"What the?" she didn't have time to solve this riddle as the voices drew nearer. Lee Ann increased her pace, plunging deeper into the forest. The path wound up and down hills until there was a fork in the trail. She thought she had put enough distance between her and the raging mob, so she hoped to throw them off by taking the spur to her left. It climbed ever upward, but the voices did not stop coming behind her and the group was not thrown off by her diversion. In fact, they were closing the gap.

Suddenly, the trail ended abruptly at the top of a cliff. Normally, this would be a place where Lee Ann would stop to take in the surroundings and marvel at the beauty around her. Instead, she was panicked at the prospect of having nowhere to retreat to. She stared out over the cliff as the stars greeted her, glinting hopefully in the void.

"Get her!" a voice cried out. Lee Ann turned around to face whomever it was. It was hard for her to make out any faces due to the dying light. Someone lunged at her, she could feel their hands on her, pushing. Her feet struggled for a foothold on the loose rocks as her hands flailed around for something to grab onto, but it was to no avail. She had fallen over the edge and could feel the air rushing up to meet her; the alarming drum of her heartbeat filled her ears as she closed her eyes.

"Mother?" she called out in alarm and distress, waking herself with the utterance.

"Are you ok?" Connor asked, looking down from her bunk opposite where Lee Ann lay covered in sweat.

"Yeah, just a bad dream," Lee Ann answered, but really, she was still alarmed, and her heartbeat had yet to slow, filling her ears with its relentless pulse.

The whole experience made Lee Ann want to get out of there and be around people and activity. She immediately got up and went to the back of the cabin towards the bathroom to get into the shower. She put on a long, black dress and tied her hair up into a ponytail, slipping on her black chucks. Connor sat with her legs draped over the side of her bunk and watched her the whole time.

"Do you have any classes today?" Lee Ann asked, to try and bring a sense of normalcy to the situation and break the awkward silence.

"Not on Mondays, my first class is tomorrow," Connor answered.

"Me, neither, but I'm feeling a bit hungry, so I'm going to try and grab some grub at the cafeteria," Lee Ann declared. "Wanna come with me? You know there's safety in numbers." Her thoughts rewound to the dream and the angry mob. She pushed it out of her thoughts immediately.

"No, I have to work up my nerve to go there," Connor allowed.

"I get it. I'll let you know how scary it is," Lee Ann joked, but the strange nature of her dream loomed in the background of her thoughts, making her uneasy.

"Ok, I'll be here!" Connor said, smiling down at her.

Lee Ann took a deep breath and exited the cabin. The sunlight shone down on her and the wind was calm, contrasting with her nightmare. She took the pebble-lined path that led towards the main part of campus, veering away from the forest to the south. Unlike the previous day, the campus was now bustling with people. There were other girls walking in the same direction and boys walking in from the opposite direction. The boy's dorms had been strategically placed on the west end of campus, as far away from the girl's dorms as possible. Anyone who dared cross the middle of campus at night would have to pass by campus security and the quarters of the head-master. Many a student had opted instead to take to the deep woods in the dead of night to cross from the east side of campus to the west.

Lee Ann looked at the girls walking near her. To her, most of the girls gave off a preppy, conservative vibe and seemed to have the best of everything- expensive jeans and shoes. Her eyes searched for anyone that might stand out- someone that might have some degree of individuality, but she couldn't find anyone. A few of the girls glanced her way and then continued to talk amongst themselves, but none of them smiled or attempted to greet her. She averted her eyes from theirs and continued to make her way across campus. A few minutes later, she had reached the mess hall, a large, wooden building with a large front porch where several groups of students were hanging out, some eating and drinking coffee and orange juice.

The doors were carved from thick oak trees and were very heavy. Lee Ann pulled with all her might, then felt the door easily open. A boy behind her grabbed the door and opened it the rest of the way for her.

"Allow me," A deep rich voice said. Lee Ann turned to see a tall, brawny guy with short dark hair and dark brown eyes. He smiled.

"Thanks," she said, shooting him a non-committal smile. She had learned over time not to be overly friendly with guys she had just met.

"You new?" he asked.

"Is it that painfully obvious?" she said as she looked around her at the large wooden farm tables that filled the main room. Beyond this was a line of students who walked behind a wooden railing, choosing their breakfast items from various food bars. The smell of eggs and sausage filled the air, reminding Lee Ann of how hungry she was.

"Kinda," he said looking her up and down quickly.

"My name's Derrick," he said, extending his hand as he smiled at her. Lee Ann shook his hand, thinking that he was handsome and rather athletic with his broad shoulders and large hands. He was not her type at all.

"Thanks, mine's Lee Ann," she responded shyly.

"Hey, so if you need anything- like how to get to a certain class or something, don't hesitate to ask me," he said. She was pleasantly surprised at his friendly demeanor. He didn't seem to be coming on to her or looking at her in an invasive way like some guys did.

"Sure, Derrick. I appreciate that," she said, finally sharing a smile with him. They locked eyes for a moment and then he walked away towards a table where about five girls sat looking at her. One of them, a tall red head with piercing blue eyes, shot her a not-so-friendly glance. Lee Ann looked away quickly, not wanting to repeat the experience she had had at Pearson High just a couple of years before.

Lee Ann got into the food line which passed very close to the table where Derrick had sat down. She moved through the line, keeping her eyes pointed towards the food selections. She took a red tray and selected a fruit salad, some scrambled eggs, and biscuits and gravy. It was the most deluxe food bar she had ever seen and would have put her old high school to shame. Although she tried her best to ignore the conversation the group was having nearby, she couldn't help but overhear the words- 'it's that girl, the one who talks to ghosts.' Lee Ann sighed, wishing that her reputation hadn't preceded her.

She sat down at a table where only a couple of groups of people were sitting, positioning herself at the far end, away from them. They looked at her and then continued their conversations, not paying her much attention. The group that sat at the table where Derrick had sat down, however, continued to stare at her and talk amongst themselves. Lee Ann tried her best to ignore them, but she couldn't help but look back at them.

Lee Ann realized she was eating quickly either because of her hunger or because she wanted to get out of there as quickly as she could. Her eyes scanned the rest of the cafeteria, looking for friendly faces. Suddenly, someone came up and sat down beside her. She was relieved to see Julie's friendly smile.

"Hey there, how are you adjusting?" Julie asked.

"Oh, ok. To tell the truth, coming in here the first time is a little intimidating. It was as if everyone in the place was looking at me, although I know that's just me being paranoid," She shared.

"I'm sure everyone feels that way when they first come- I know I did," Julie answered, comforting Lee Ann with her empathetic words.

"That's good to know." Lee Ann took a deep breath that was more of a sigh of relief at the sight of a friend.

"So, do you need any help figuring out your schedule or the locations of any of your classes?" Julie inquired.

"I think I'm good. I studied the campus map yesterday so that I would know where to go," She revealed.

"Excellent! Well, gotta go. I have another campus tour to conduct in about ten minutes," Julie said as she gazed at her Apple watch to check the time.

"Cool, see you around, and thanks for everything. Thanks for… for being so nice," Lee Ann answered, hoping that she didn't' sound too strange.

"Hey, don't mention it. See you soon!" Julie said with her characteristic ear to ear grin.

"See ya!" Lee Ann answered with a smile. The whole exchange left Lee Ann feeling better, like she wasn't a pariah after all.

Then, a group of girls that had been sitting at the table with Derrick got up and walked past her table slowly. She tried her best to ignore them but couldn't help but overhear a short blonde girl whisper to the redhead, the word, 'freak.' It was a trigger word for Lee Ann that harkened back to the Pearson High days and her encounters with Mary Hartford and her henchwomen. She shook her head, feeling as if she were repeating her revolting high school experience all over again.

"Hello to you, too!" Lee Ann had tried to avoid confrontation, but she'd been through too much to allow these snobby girls to treat her this way. She looked at them to let them know she wasn't intimidated.

"Did someone say something to you?" the redhead asked in a caustic voice.

"No, I guess you don't have the guts to confront me directly. If you have something to say to me, I'm here," Lee Ann shot back. The others seemed shocked at her directness as if they were used to whispering about people and getting away with it.

The redhead laughed and walked over to the table, standing over Lee Ann.

"Look, ghosthunter girl. I'm not sure why you decided to come to Farthington, but take come smart advice from me. Stay away from us, freak!"

"Gladly, but to answer your question- I came here because I

heard that the best and brightest come here. I guess I'll find them at some point." The redhead glared at her and balled her fists.

Lee Ann straightened her back and prepared to fight back if necessary.

"No, but seriously, why would some freak come to a school where she isn't wanted, where she doesn't fit in and won't find acceptance?"

"Looks like someone is stuck in high school. Ever think it might be time to broaden your horizons and come out of your fantasy world full of designer clothes and shallow viewpoints?" The girl didn't answer back, instead, she took a cup full of ice and threw it at Lee Ann, who shot up from her seat. The redhead jumped backwards and ran off with the others following behind her. She could her them all laughing amongst themselves. A custodial worker frowned and ran up to begin cleaning up the ice.

Lee Ann felt so disgusted that she couldn't finish her biscuits and gravy. She threw them into the trash and made for the door. Several people watched her exit, but none of them said anything to her, preferring to whisper amongst themselves about the proceedings. For the remainder of the day, she was on constant guard should one of the unpleasant girls cross her path. She managed to steer clear of them until the end of the day when the redhead and one of her friends spotted Lee Ann as she walked back towards the dorms.

"Gonna do any ghost hunting tonight?" she heard the girl say, but she decided to ignore her and quickened her pace instead.

Not even a long walk in the woods and some time with her sketchbook made her forget what happened that morning.

SIX

WATCHER FROM THE WOODS

When Lee Ann got back to the dorm, she immediately went to her bed and lay down on her stomach, burying her face in her pillow.

"Are you alright?" Connor asked from her bunk as she put down the book she was reading.

Lee Ann looked up at her with the same look of disgust she had during the incident at the cafeteria.

"I can't believe I came all this way just to have the same treatment that I suffered through back in high school. They should warn you in the campus brochures, 'Warning, new students may encounter unfriendly snob monsters!'

'That's another reason why I didn't want to go to the cafeteria, especially after the looks I got from some of the girls when I first arrived."

Lee Ann balled her fists and turned over on her back, continuing her tirade as if she hadn't heard a word Connor had just spoken.

"I swear, why did I let my dad convince me to come here? I could have had a full ride at art school. But no, I must pursue an education that will lead to some lifeless desk job!"

"You don't have to do that. You will be an artist. I mean, you are an artist, and they can't take that away from you," Connor stated with a sympathetic smile that softened Lee Ann's mood a bit.

"Thanks Connor. You know, I'm lucky to have you as my room-mate. What would have happened if one of those snobby trolls had been assigned to this cabin? We might have murdered one another before the term even started." They both began to laugh at the thought of this scenario.

"Don't worry, I got your back," Connor said, giving Lee Ann a sense of reassurance, she hadn't felt since she met David, Jasmine, and Katrina.

Lee Ann stretched, yawned, and pulled the sheet up to her chin.

"Well, I think that I suffered through enough drama for one day. Goodnight!" she said as she rolled to one side.

"Good night!" Connor answered.

BACK AT THE MESS HALL, the group of girls that Lee Ann had encountered were talking.

"I swear, if I see her talking to Derrick again, I don't know what I'll do," the redhead declared.

"Don't worry, Gina, Derrick would never leave you for someone like her," The short blonde declared.

"Thanks Claire, but you saw the way he was looking at her. I know how a guy looks at a girl when he's attracted to her. Anyway, I better get back to the dorm. Orientation is first thing in the morning, and I don't want to sleep through it."

"Ok, see ya," Claire answered as she and the other two girls walked off together.

Gina looked up at the sky that had been lit up by the moon just minutes before. As soon as the others were gone, it was as if a veil had been drawn across the moon ensuring that she would have to find her way back in the dark. She nervously made her way down the rocky path towards the edge of the forest. There wasn't even a slight breeze to disrupt the quiet. The crunch of Gina's shoes on the pebbles seemed abnormally loud. She wished she could muffle the sound. After taking another step, Gina paused, thinking that she heard something move in the forest. She peered into the gloom between the staunch silhouettes of the trees but couldn't make out anything.

"Probably just an animal," She whispered to herself as she quickened her pace.

In her peripheral vision, she could sense movement again in the adjacent forest. Something seemed to move when she moved and stop when she stopped.

"Alright, Claire, Becky, and Laura, that better not be you or I'm going to be pissed!" she said, hoping this would make her feel brave. However, no one answered, and her words seemed to get swallowed up by the forest. She didn't like the awful stillness and quiet that followed, so she began to jog towards the cabin, which she could now see just a couple hundred yards ahead.

She paused a few yards and leaned against a tree to catch her breath when something caught her eye just a few yards into the trees. A menacing pair of glowing eyes stared back at her and then vanished. Gina's heart began to pound as she broke into a run and did her best not to panic. She did not dare to look over towards the forest but focused on the friendly white lights outside her cabin. Her hyper focus kept her from seeing a large stone in her path that tripped her and caused her to fall onto her belly, thankfully onto the grass. She could feel the eyes on her again as she struggled to get to her feet. It was as if some force was making it difficult to move, like there had been a large weight placed on her back.

"Help! Ahhh!" she called out as her feet thrashed about in the grass. Finally, she was able to get up and began moving forward again. As much as she wanted to look away, she couldn't help but gaze back into the forest. There were those sick eyes again, looking into her own with a rage that was so powerful, Gina couldn't look away. She could make out the silhouette of a tall figure, but it was too dark to make out any other defining characteristics.

"Who are you?" Gina managed to cry out, but the figure vanished. The spell of its rage seemed to lift as Gina managed to run the last few yards to the front door of the cabin. She fumbled with her keys, still feeling the presence of the figure in the woods. As she turned the key in the door, she took one last look over her shoulder. There, at the edge of the woods, but still obscured by the darkness was the tall figure again. This time, Gina could see that it was a girl with long hair, but only the glowing eyes gave any hint to her facial features. Gina wanted to scream, to curse at the girl for scaring her, but instead her lips trembled, and her palms filled with sweat as she struggled to fit the key in the door. The girl's feet were not touching the ground! Finally, the key turned in the doorknob and the door flung open. Gina got inside, closed the door quickly and looked out of the window. The figure at the edge of the woods was nowhere to be seen.

"Are you ok?" Becky immediately asked her, alarmed by the wide-eyed expression on Gina's face.

"I think so. There was something or someone out there in the woods...." Gina stammered.

Becky and Claire looked at each other and then back at Gina. They had never seen her like this before. She was usually stoic and level-headed.

"I don't know how to describe it, but it was a girl, I think. I'm not sure. I just know that whoever or whatever it was following me. I'm going to talk to campus security tomorrow."

"What did she look like?" Becky asked.

"I couldn't make her out all that well in the dark."

After a slight pause Becky responded, "Maybe it was Cassie."

"Who the hell is Cassie?" Gina asked, sounding a bit more like her old self.

"You mean you haven't heard the story?" she asked them as she pushed her long, straight blonde hair behind her shoulders. Her hazel eyes sparkled with mystery.

"No, do tell," Claire added.

"Well supposedly back in the late seventies, there was a girl that went to school her named Cassie. Apparently, she didn't fit in very well and was miserable. In fact, she was so miserable, she jumped from the top of Whispering Falls. The rumor is that she now wanders the woods looking for the girls that tormented her."

"Sounds like a great campfire story," Gina replied in her usual stoic manner. However, her hands were trembling slightly as she thought about her recent experience. She wasn't one to believe stories like this, but her mind pictured the girl whose feet didn't touch the ground and those eyes- those sickly, glowing eyes.

"That's a creepy story and all, but we all need to get to bed. Don't forget that orientation is first thing in the morning," Claire reminded them.

Gina lay in her bed staring at the ceiling, trying not to look out of the nearby window for fear of seeing the girl again.

CHAPTER
SEVEN
ESCALATION

The next morning, Lee Ann woke up to her alarm clock, not feeling completely rested. She knew she had some interesting dreams the previous night but couldn't recall what they were no matter how hard she tried. Connor was already up fixing some coffee. She was dressed in her usual shorts and black t-shirt.

"Hey, sleep well?" Connor asked her.

"Thanks for asking, but for some reason I didn't sleep very soundly. I guess I need to get used to being here. Hey Connor, can I ask you something?"

"Sure," Connor said with a smile.

"Do you think there are any other people like us at this school?"

"Eh, well as far as I can tell probably not but I haven't exactly met that many people to be fair," Connor admitted.

"True. It's just the vibe I get off this place.. that it doesn't welcome individualism. I feel like it's pre-programming the students for a pre-programmed life."

"Guess I haven't thought about it like that, but I guess you're right," Connor agreed as she stirred some cream into her coffee.

"So, you goin' to orientation?" Lee Ann asked.

"No, I already went through it," Connor quickly answered. Lee Ann was puzzled, not knowing that this was an option.

"Oh, when?"

"When I first got here," Connor answered, not offering any further explanation.

Lee Ann wanted to ask more questions about this, but she looked at the time and saw that she only had thirty minutes before orientation began. She got up and made for the shower. With only minutes to spare, she slid on the floral-print dress her mother had picked out for her the year that she passed and slid on her combat boots. Connor was back in her bunk reading a book.

"I'm off, see you later!" Lee Ann said as she headed for the door.

"Bye!" Connor answered. As she made for the main office where orientation was to begin, she did her best to try and forget the events of the previous day to give herself a clean slate. Surely there were others like her and Connor or at least other students who wouldn't treat her like some pariah. As she walked, she spotted Derrick walking in the same direction from the east. He spotted her and gave her a wave. She waved back shyly, glancing around to make sure that Gina and the other girls weren't around.

"Hey, morning!" Derrick said, making his way towards her.

"Morning," She answered noncommittally.

"Look I just wanted to say sorry again for the way my girlfriend treated you yesterday. It wasn't cool," he said, stopping beside her.

"It wasn't your fault. Is she usually that jealous?"

"It isn't the first time, but she is a different person when you get her one on one, I swear," he said, sounding like he was trying to justify his own relationship.

"I'll have to take your word on that," Lee Ann said as they began to walk towards the main office.

"I also just wanted to say that I'm glad that Farthington has some new blood- someone unique and special. You are an internet celebrity. I heard about that situation in, eh...."

"Laverne?"

"Yeah, Laverne. I heard it was all haunted in the woods around there and you stopped it somehow. Is it true and if so, how did you do it?"

"That's a loaded question. The truth is, I'm trying to distance myself from that whole thing. I guess you could say I have a gift or maybe a curse depending on how you look at it. If you believe in that sort of thing, I can see spirits and communicate with them. I simply helped them to see that it was time for them to move on..."

"Move onto what?"

"The next life I suppose."

"Wow, fascinating!" Derrick said as a flash of wonder mixed with an undeniable attraction towards Lee Ann moved across his face. Lee Ann looked away again, sensing this. As she did, her eyes landed on Gina and her friends who were also moving in the same direction. Gina was staring daggers at them, having noticed that her boyfriend was with Lee Ann.

"GOTTA GO, SEE YOU LATER!" Derrick said, not looking at Lee Ann as if it had only been coincidence that he had been walking beside her.

Lee Ann watched from a distance as Gina fussed at him. She knew he was getting a tongue-lashing for talking to her, and she thought again how much she hated her father at that moment for not allowing her to go to art school. She looked at the schedule that she had printed off and saw that the orientation was to begin in the student life hall. As she took off in that direction, Gina suddenly appeared in front of her with her arms crossed.

"What do you want?" Lee Ann asked, unable to hide her annoyance.

"I'm here to give you a warning, freak. Do not talk to my man ever again!" Gina announced as she balled up her hands into fists.

"He came up to me and started talking for your information. He was just being polite, which is something you should investigate some time, might take you far in life!"

Gina scowled, grinded her teeth and took a step towards Lee Ann who didn't move an inch from her position. Without her friends there to back her up, Gina was unwilling to make another move. For a moment, Gina recalled the figure in the woods that had been stalking her although she wasn't sure why she thought of it. Somehow, Lee Ann's appearance before her conjured up the memory. Her face revealed the unease that it called to her mind.

"That's what I thought," Lee Ann said, calling her bluff.

"Just remember what I said. Stay away from Derrick or else we will work extra hard to make sure that you don't feel welcome here!" Gina said, regaining her anger as she pushed the memory of the unpleasant encounter out of her mind.

Lee Ann refused to dignify her threat with a response, electing instead to roll her eyes and walk past her towards the student life building. Gina hated more than anything to be ignored; she pushed Lee Ann just as she walked past her. Lee Ann fell to the ground on her back, dropping her books. Gina laughed and ran away from her. Lee Ann took off running after her, determined to show Gina that she was not going to be intimidated and that there would be consequences every time she was bullied. However, Gina used to run track in high school and was able to outrun her. She reached her cabin and slammed and locked the door before Lee Ann could get to her.

"Coward!" Lee Ann yelled through the door, hearing giggles coming from inside.

THAT NIGHT, Gina awoke from a dead sleep, feeling unnaturally cold for an early September evening in the south. Although she was unsure why, she was compelled to get up and look out of the window. The moonlight was streaming in and was suddenly obscured by a lone cloud that moved past it. Gina stared out into the gloom of the tree line behind the cabin as something big moved quickly across her field of vision. She felt uneasy and afraid no matter how much she tried to be brave.

Suddenly, she heard a tapping sound, like footsteps on the front porch. Gina moved to the door and wondered what to do. Should she wake the others? Was there a prowler sneaking around the woods? Then her mind went to the story that Becky had told them recently about Cassie. She shook her head to remind herself that she didn't believe in such nonsense. As she moved towards the door, she took a deep breath to try and gather all her courage. Her fear gave way to anger as she thought of her encounter with Lee Ann earlier that day.

She's trying to scare me, but I'll show her that she's the one who should be scared.

The sound of the footsteps ceased as Gina stopped at the door, trying to muster the courage to open it. After taking another deep breath, she threw the door open and prepared to face the person at the door. There was no one there and the night seemed impossibly still and quiet, draining Gina of the courage she had managed to gather. She managed to open her mouth to speak, feeling like it took an immense amount of effort, like the way one feels when there is an urge to cry out in a dream, but cannot for some reason.

"Who... who's there? Lee Ann, that better not be you!"

For what seemed like an eternity, there was no response. Gina could feel the heavy warm air of the late summer give way to a cool breeze that blew through her hair. The breeze seemed to stir some leaves on the front porch into a whirlwind. Within moments, a shadowy figure seemed to be conjured up. Gina's heart began to pound as she took a fearful step backwards into the cabin. The shadow moved towards her, suddenly taking human form. Although Gina couldn't make out the facial features, she knew she had encountered this person or whatever it was just a few nights' prior, seeing the outline of a girl.

"Lee Ann?" her voice trembled, revealing her fear. The figure lunged forward, making a hissing sound that seemed to surround the entire cabin revealing the same glowing, angry eyes as before.

Gina took another step backwards as a strong wind blew around the cabin and slammed the door, knocking Gina backwards onto the floor. The sound awakened Becky and Claire who sat up in bed and looked at Gina's body on the floor in front of the door in puzzlement.

"Are you alright, Gina? What happened?" Claire asked as she got to her feet and offered her hand. Gina took her hand and stood up. She was breathing hard and had a large welt on her forehead where the door had hit her.

"It was that Lee Ann; I just know it!" Gina declared as her fear was overcome by anger.

LEE ANN MOVED through the woods, not knowing where she was headed in that moment. All that she knew was that urgency was needed- someone or something was in pursuit of her. Then the voices ushered from some place behind her in the forest.

"She's taking the spur to the top of the falls!" a female voice cried out. The trees echoed the voice, making it sound much closer.

Then, Lee Ann realized where she was. All at once the trail ended at the overlook. Keeping her distance from the edge, she turned to survey her options. She could now see the shadowy outline of the people approaching, both from the main trail and the spur she had just come off. There was nowhere to go. She turned towards the edge and stared down at the grotto, getting lost for a moment in the rushing sound of the ever-falling water. A male voice spoke out as the figures crept closer causing her to turn around. In the process, she lost her footing, falling forward. Her legs dangled over the edge of the cliff, just a couple of feet from the rushing water of the falls. She reached for the protruding root of a nearby tree pulling herself away from the precipice, just as she awoke. Only she was not in her bed; she was asleep only inches away from edge of the cliff, next to the falls. Upon waking, she gasped and moved backwards causing rocks to tumble over the edge as her feet shuffled along the ground.

"Am I still dreaming?" she asked herself, pinching her arm in the process. The nighttime scene around her did not change. She did her best to catch her breath, reminding herself that she had seen and lived through some strange things in her day, however young she might be. Nonetheless, she had no idea what was happening to her, and her thoughts traveled out to her mother, Felicity, and of course, David. She steadied her breath as she made her way out of the forest and to the light on the front porch of her cabin. Connor was awake when she entered.

"Are you ok? Where did you go?" she asked, looking concerned.

"Yeah, thankfully. Look, I don't want to freak you out, but I just woke up at the edge of the waterfall!"

"What? Gosh! I'm so glad you're ok. You must have sleep-walked or something. Have you ever done anything like that before?"

"No, never. I mean, don't get me wrong, I am 'Lee Ann the Teenage Loop Breaker' and all that garbage, but I've never been through anything like this before. It's so very similar to my first dream. A group of people were chasing me both times. In each instance, it's nighttime and I'm at the edge of the waterfall. If I hadn't awoken, I would have gone over the edge again just like in the first dream. Something happened there, and as much as I don't want to be bothered with this sort of thing anymore, I'm going to have to figure out what it was. Besides, how can I be expected to focus on my studies with this kind of stuff happening?"

"I agree, you should find out if anything happened around here. Maybe someone is trying to send you a message or show you something." Connor replied.

THE NEXT MORNING, Lee Ann did her best to pull herself together and attend her classes at the college. The first was an art history class with Dr. Kendall. On her way across the main quad, she spotted Gina and her friends, making sure to give them a wide berth. She was close enough to overhear them.

"I'm telling you it was Cassie," Becky insisted, betraying a touch of sarcasm in her tone.

"No, there is no Cassie. There is just Lee Ann. Look, we must make it known that she is not welcome here. I'm telling you that freak is trying to scare me. She stalked me in the woods. Then, she appeared just outside the cabin. She slammed the door and did this to me, Gina said pointing at her forehead.

The others looked at Gina in doubt.

"How did she shut the door from such a long distance away?" Claire asked Gina. There was an uncomfortable silence that followed as they all contemplated this.

"Look, I don't know how she did it, but she did. I'm not going to just lay down and take it either!" Gina declared.

CHAPTER
EIGHT
I HEARD A RUMOR

L ee Ann decided to take a longer way around to the lecture hall to avoid Gina and her friends. However, her interest was piqued at the mention of this 'Cassie' person. She was anxious for an opportunity to get Becky alone and find out more if she could. Lee Ann was so preoccupied with all that had taken place, she was unable to focus on Dr. Kendall's introductory lecture about the importance of Art History in modern society and its continued place as the 'cultural soul' of our existence.

After the class was over, she decided to try and return to the cafeteria and get something to eat even though that might mean another risk of having a run in with Gina. She entered the building, grabbed a tray, and looked at the various lines. There was a salad bar to her left and grilled items to her right. She opted for the salad bar line and immediately spotted Becky. There was no sign of Gina, Claire, or any of the other girls she remembered from the last encounter. As soon as Becky reached the end of the line, Lee Ann went over to her, giving up her place in the line.

"Hey!" she said in her most friendly voice. Becky shot her a look of annoyance.

"What do you want?" she asked suspiciously.

"Look, I know we didn't get off on the right foot, but I just wanted to talk to you, alone," Lee Ann shared. Becky looked around to see if her friends could see them, ran a finger through her curly bob haircut and motioned for her to follow her to one of the outside tables near the exit.

Becky sat down at a table, scanned the area once more and then motioned for Lee Ann to join her.

"Can't be seen talking to the freak, eh?" Lee Ann teased.

"Look, I don't have anything against you personally, but you can't keep trying to scare Gina. You should have seen the look on her face last night. I couldn't tell if she was mad or frightened out of her wits!"

"What? It wasn't me; I was asleep in my cabin. You can ask my roommate, Connor," Lee Ann insisted. Becky could tell by the look on Lee Ann's face that she wasn't lying. Becky took another look around her to make sure the coast was clear before answering,

"Do you know about the story of Cassie and Katie?" Becky asked.

"No, who are they?"

"You mean who were they. They were two girls that went to school here in the seventies who ended up committing suicide here on campus," Becky shared.

"Oh my god! How?" Lee Ann inquired.

"They jumped over the falls..." Becky said, swallowing hard as soon as the words left her mouth.

Lee Ann's face went white as she thought back to her dreams and to that very morning when she had awoken at the edge of the falls. She knew at that point that she was being contacted and shown something, but she wasn't sure what. It was the last thing that she had wanted to get mixed up in, but she knew that she had to figure it out or it would continue and make it next to impossible for her to focus on her course work.

"If I tell you something, will you promise to keep it between us?" Lee Ann said. Becky was moved by the look on Lee Ann's face. She realized in that moment that Lee Ann was not some weirdo, but someone who was genuinely frightened and concerned about what was happening.

"Sure, go ahead," Becky said, leaning in.

"I have been having dreams about being chased to the edge of a waterfall. I also saw the silhouette of someone falling over the falls when my roommate and I hiked to the bottom of Whispering Falls, but here's the strangest thing- I woke up near the edge of the falls this morning after having another dream about being chased. I guess I must have sleepwalked there. As you probably know, I've had some experience with, um, the beyond, and this has that written all over it."

"Oh my god, she's probably trying to contact you!" Becky said. It was obvious that she believed in this sort of thing much more than her friends.

"Well, if there is a spiritual presence here, I would probably be the one that it tries to contact. You see, people like me who have certain abilities to see spirits or whatever you want to call them are kind of like homing beacons for restless spirits. Many times, they don't even know they have passed on and they are seeking help or guidance. We try to help them see that they need to move on and let go of whatever they are holding onto that is keeping them bound to this plane of existence."

"Move on to where, the next plane or something?"

"Exactly. I'm only just beginning to understand it all myself, believe it or not."

"Maybe Cassie or Katie, whichever it might be, doesn't know they have passed on and they are seeking your help for some reason."

"That's entirely possible. Either way, I wonder why this Cassie or Katie, whomever it is wants to threaten Gina," Lee Ann mused.

"I know, maybe she wants to defend you. Maybe she doesn't like how Gina is treating you," Becky stated. She no longer seemed to care if anyone overheard them or not. Lee Ann began to feel that she could trust her.

"Will you help convince Gina that it isn't me who is trying to stalk her? Honestly, it feels like she just had it in for me since day one."

"Well, if you haven't noticed she's a bit jealous and insecure, though I love her. We've known each other since middle school, and believe it or not, she has another side. Seeing how friendly Derrick was to you got you off on the wrong foot- well that and the whole 'ghost girl' thing."

"Believe it or not, I'm trying to get away from that. I never asked for any 'gifts' like that or whatever. I just want to pursue my art and get on with my life."

"Maybe it's just something you can't run from?" Becky pointed out. Lee Ann thought about this for a moment, then she realized that she was about to be late for her English class.

"Gotta go, but I'd like to talk again soon," Lee Ann said.

"Yeah, sure, I'll do what I can on my end. Good luck figuring out what's going on. Who knows, maybe it will all just stop." Becky smiled and turned to leave. Lee Ann could see Gina and Claire coming over the hill. Becky hurried towards them, trying not to look like she'd been talking with Lee Ann.

"Were you talking to her?" Gina asked, unable to hide the disdain in her voice.

"She talked to me," Becky said defensively.

"Doesn't mean you have to talk back," Claire answered. Becky shot her a cold glance.

"She insisted that she wasn't at our cabin the other night and I believe her," Becky stated. The others looked aghast.

"What? C'mon Becky, don't give me that ghost crap again. She did it and quite frankly you're a sucker if you believe her. Why can't she be brave enough to just admit it?" Gina began to pace back and forth causing Claire and Becky to look at one another with concern.

"Let's just report her to campus security and if that doesn't work, we'll ask for a meeting with the headmaster!" Claire insisted.

"No, that's not good enough. Maybe we should give her a dose of her own medicine," Gina suggested. Claire and Becky looked at each other again, but they both knew that once Gina got started down this path, she was not easy to sway. They had not seen her this worked up since she challenged her ex-boyfriend's new girlfriend for a fight in the middle of the hallway back in high school.

Lee Ann came back to the cabin after class. Connor looked as if she had never even moved from her bunk bed the entire day.

"Did you go to class today?" Lee Ann inquired.

"Didn't feel well, so I missed my classes. I let the professors know, though."

"Oh, I hope you're feeling better."

"I am now, thanks!" Connor said as she kicked her legs over the edge of the bunk.

"Have you ever heard about Cassie and Katie?" Lee Ann blurted out. Connor's eyes widened but she did not reply right away.

"Yes, I have heard the story," Connor finally spoke.

"Well, I think that one of them is trying to contact me or show me something. That's why I keep having these dreams and why I saw someone go over the falls. I've got to figure out what it is she's trying to tell me," Lee Ann explained. Connor smiled, jumped down from her bunk bed and stood beside Lee Ann.

"I'll help you!" Connor insisted.

"Great. I guess we can start by finding out as much as we can about what happened to them and by trying to contact them to communicate with them if we can. However, I want to get some advice from a trusted friend before we try that. Making contact can be dangerous in certain circumstances," Lee Ann explained. It was Felicity she was thinking about, and she was glad that there was a Labor Day holiday coming up very soon to allow her to return home and get some good advice.

"Sounds like a great plan!" Connor said with a smile.

Lee Ann fell asleep reading her Art History textbook while Connor listened to the Clash and tapped her toes against the side of the bedframe to the music. Suddenly a loud cracking noise that was louder than Connor's footwork was heard just outside the front door. It was loud enough to wake up Lee Ann who lay there and listened. A second cracking sound was heard, like a branch being snapped, but this time it sounded closer and louder.

Lee Ann looked up at Connor and they locked eyes for a moment as if they were speaking telepathically. Connor quietly climbed down.

"What do you think that is?" Lee Ann whispered.

"I don't know," Connor answered, also whispering.

"I'm going to have a look outside," Lee Ann answered. She crept towards the door, slowly unlatched the deadbolt, grabbed the doorknob, and quickly opened the door. There was no one there and no movement or sound other than the crickets and the occasional gust of wind. Lee Ann stepped out onto the stone porch and looked out into the gloom. A shape moved near the edge of the forest in her peripheral vision. She turned towards the forest, hearing something crunching the leaves on the woodland floor. Lee Ann got out her cell phone, turned on the flashlight and ran after the sound. Once inside the forest, the sound stopped.

"Hello? Who is out here?" Lee Ann asked. For what seemed like an eternity there was silence and then came an answer issuing from behind a large oak.

"Caaaaaassssssssie," a whispery voice answered. It was more of a hiss than a whisper.

Lee Ann looked down at her hands. They were not trembling as they should have been in the presence of something supernatural, which struck her as interesting. Then, before Lee Ann could answer, two shapes emerged from behind two nearby trees. Lee Ann took a step backwards, not knowing what she was about to face. She tripped on a root and fell onto her back. The shapes now stood over on either side of her menacingly, but Lee Ann could now see that it was Gina and Claire. Gina took a quick picture of Lee Ann's shocked expression as she and Claire began to laugh.

"This should really be humiliating when I post it on Tik Tok," Gina remarked.

Lee Ann quickly got on her feet; the two friends laughed and began to run away from her through the woods. When they were about to reach the clearing, the sound of a woman's echoey laughter filled the woods all around them. Lee Ann could hear it too; she looked down at her hands which had begun to tremble. She continued to run after Gina and Claire, but they had broken into a sprint when they heard the laughter and were gone. Lee Ann stopped at the edge of the wood to speak to the voice.

"Hello!" Who are you? What do you need to show me?" Lee Ann inquired, but only the crickets answered her with their hypnotic chorus.

NINE

MENDING THE TIES

L ee Ann could not wait to get back home for the Labor Day holiday. She needed a break from whatever was happening, and she needed an outside perspective, especially Felicity's. In the last couple of weeks, her grades had taken a tumble due mainly to the distraction of the unexplained events taking place. The only class that she currently had an 'A' in was Art History. This stood in stark contrast to the high marks she earned throughout high school. Despite her best efforts, she could not motivate herself to take a deeper interest in the required courses she had been advised to take. She dreaded having to face that disappointed smirk on her father's face and the inevitable declarations of his disappointment. Lee Ann could picture him standing there with his arms crossed in a sanctimonious posture. Then there was David—poor David. She had been so preoccupied that she had neglected to answer more than a couple of the texts he had sent late at night. Lee Ann had realized this and sent him an apologetic text a couple of days ago, letting him know that she was coming home for the holiday. He didn't answer back.

Lee Ann was happy to see Charles drive up in the same old red

Chevy pickup. He even had the same Caterpillar cap and vest jacket. She grinned, thinking of him as frozen in time like a museum mannequin who you can always count on to appear the same, donning the same clothes.

"Hey Punkin!" he shouted as he opened the door of the truck.

"Hey Dad," Lee Ann answered, less enthusiastically. Her irritation came flooding back as she recalled how it was her father's fault that she was at Farthington in the first place. Nonetheless, she did hug him back when he extended his arms. The warmth and the tobacco mixed with the leathery smell of her father gave her reassurance; it made her long for them to be home.

After this moment of affection, Lee Ann clammed up again, choosing to gaze at the passing trees as they drove towards the highway. She swallowed, dreading the inevitable inquisition that was surely coming.

"So, everything is going well so far?" he asked after about twenty minutes of awkward silence.

"About as good as can be expected," she answered, unable to hide the sarcasm in her voice.

"Now, what is that supposed to mean?"

"It means that it could be going better. The girls there all hate me, my grades are mediocre, and some spirit is trying to contact me. How's your last few weeks been?"

Charles glanced over at her concernedly and took a deep breath.

"Well, that's a lot to take in. When you say mediocre grades, how mediocre are we talking about here?" Charles continued.

"You see, that's just what I suspected. What about the fact that I don't fit in and I'm miserable? Doesn't that mean anything to you?" Lee Ann's anger came flooding out, surprising even her.

"Of course I care! We just can't have you flunking out of school when you're a straight 'A' student! Christ, Lee Ann you've got to keep your focus and not let some snobby girls mess up your mojo."

"It's not as simple as that, and besides, I didn't say I was flunking anything," Lee Ann's voice began to crack with emotion. "You don't know what it's like to have to deal with being contacted by the dead while at the same time dealing with living people who don't want you around. It's no picnic."

"I'm sorry, punk'in. I just want you to realize your fullest potential because I know what you're capable of," he expressed. Lee Ann softened a bit when she saw the care in his eyes. He pulled out a handkerchief and handed it to her. A few tears were beginning to run down Lee Ann's cheek.

"Who still carries around handkerchiefs?" Lee Ann asked. Charles laughed, breaking the tension.

"Just me, I guess," he answered. Lee Ann smiled, but deep down she still held some resentment towards him for the current situation.

Lee Ann was beyond happy to see the gate for their property along Green Creek Road. She was also pleased to see Shirley walking up towards the gate to greet them. She looked slimmer and happier to Lee Ann. Shirley had been on a huge exercise kick lately and would go out walking for miles.

"Oh my god, you look so great!" Lee Ann said, throwing her arms around her stepmom as soon as she emerged from the truck.

"Thanks dear, you do too!" Shirley responded, hugging her back. She wondered to herself why Lee Ann's eye makeup was running.

"Is everything alright?" Shirley asked, looking first at Lee Ann and then to Charles.

"Yeah, everything's fine," Charles reassured her, but Shirley could tell that he wasn't revealing everything.

That night, Lee Ann told Shirley and Charles everything that had transpired, including all the strange events of the last few weeks.

"Bless your heart- you just can't get away from it, can you?" Shirley asked. Charles shot her a look as if to suggest he thought she should be more critical. It was an interesting turn of events that Lee Ann couldn't help but take mental note of.

"So, are you planning on bringing up these, um, grades then?" Charles dared to ask.

"Yes, dad! Haven't you heard anything that I've said? How much would you be able to focus on your studies if all of what I told you was happening to you?" she reasoned.

"She's right, dear. You know Lee Ann isn't a slacker. There's a good reason why she's not doing as well as she's accustomed to," Shirley said in her defense. Lee Ann smiled, thinking how odd it was that Shirley, who used to not understand her was now her staunchest defender. Charles didn't answer; instead, he gazed out of the window as if he were wishing himself away.

Lee Ann went up to her old room, checking her phone as she walked up the stairs to see if David had answered her text that she sent him when she arrived in Laverne. He had read it, but he hadn't responded.

I love you, good night! I want to see you as soon as you can!! she texted. She lay on her bed staring at her phone for a while to see if he would respond, but he never did. Feelings of guilt began to hound her as she thought of all the times she should have responded more quickly to David. Eventually, she fell asleep with the phone in her hand.

The next morning, she awoke as her phone vibrated; it was Felicity calling her.

"Hey! I'm so glad you're here! Would you like to meet for breakfast this morning so we can catch up?" Felicity asked with a tone so joyous, it lifted Lee Ann's spirits.

"Yes! How about Brian's Breakfast Shack?" Felicity suggested.

"Where else in this tiny town can you get a decent breakfast?" Lee Ann asked, recalling how flakey and delicious the homemade biscuits were.

As she got ready, she frowned to see that David still had not answered any of her texts, although he had read them. She had plans to see Jasmine and Katrina later that evening and hoped that she could convince David to join them. Lee Ann elected to walk to town like she used to, allowing memories to come flooding back as she saw the familiar buildings of Laverne- the post office, the grocery store: all frozen in time like nothing had happened at all since she'd left there. She could feel the eyes of the locals looking at her with recognition. An elder couple whispered to one another as she walked by. Lee Ann smiled because it was such a familiar situation for her when she walked through town.

Felicity was already waiting for her in a booth at the back of the café, away from prying ears. Lee Ann thought she looked happy and . The mere sight of her familiar floral-print dress and empathetic smile filled Lee Ann with reassurance. Felicity got up and gave her a long, loving hug. Lee Ann could feel her loving warmth but she could also tell that Felicity was taking in her essence and picking up on her troubles.

"How are you my dear?" she asked, and Lee Ann could tell right away that she was concerned by the crease in her forehead and the tone of her voice.

"Not so great as you can probably tell. I can't seem to focus on my studies, I don't fit in at all, I get bullied like I'm in high school again, and as if all of that wasn't enough, I now have a restless spirit trying to tell me something. Just a typical year in the life of Lee Ann."

Felicity laughed, grasped Lee Ann's hand more tightly and smiled. Her warm grip and compassionate glance gave Lee Ann comfort.

"I can sense such great... anger in you. I can feel it seething up from deep within. It keeps you anxious and unfocused," Felicity shared.

"Yes, I'm angry at the whole situation, but especially at my dad. I keep coming back to the fact that I would be much happier in art school than at Farthington, and it was dad that insisted I go there."

"I see. Do you think you could forgive him for doing what he believes is best for you? Maybe if you focus on his intentions, it will make you a little less angry with him," Felicity suggested.

"I see what you mean, but I'm eighteen now and it's time for him to let me make my own decisions, especially considering I got a scholarship and he's not paying for it," Lee Ann reasoned.

"I understand your perspective, but the anger you feel is only harming you. You must try and let go of it. Although it may not be clear to you now, at this moment, your anger is the obstacle at the heart of everything," Felicity stated.

Lee Ann took a deep breath. She knew that Felicity was right, but she wasn't fully ready to let go.

"Let's talk about this spirit you say is trying to tell you something," Felicity suggested.

Lee Ann went on to tell Felicity about everything that had been occurring: the night at the falls, the dreams, and the visitations at Gina's cabin. Felicity's expression looked increasingly concerned as Lee Ann filled her in on the details; she thought long and hard after Lee Ann finished before speaking again.

"Have you found out more about Cassie and Katie, the ones that people say committed suicide?" Felicity inquired.

"I only just heard the stories about it, but that was going to be my next move once I got a break from school. I thought of researching it several times, but to tell the truth, I tried to push the whole situation out of my mind in a failed attempt to try and focus on my schoolwork," Lee Ann shared.

Felicity took her laptop out of a large cloth bag that sat in the booth next to her. She came over to Lee Ann's side of the booth so that they could look at the computer together.

The first thing that they unearthed was a newspaper article about a punk suicide cult at Farthington from the late seventies. The article stated that Cassie Burton and Katie Connors were friends and roommates at Farthington and that were the subject of taunts and bullying which led to them jumping over the falls. Cassie jumped first, in the early evening hours of November 6, 1978, and Katie jumped from the same location five days later, on the 11th. The bodies were both found downstream from the site, washed up on gravel bars. The police did not acknowledge the theory that this might have been part of a cult as there was no evidence of it. The article was succinct and not long on details.

After a little more probing, they found an article in the local paper about a mysterious fire in one of the dormitory cabins at Farthington, a year later in 1979. The cabin burned to the ground and the occupants barely escaped with their lives. The police could not find the origin of the fire and ruled it an accident, possibly due to rodents chewing the wiring or some other cause. When the police interviewed the girls who were staying in the dorm, they say they saw the outline of a girl standing near the doorway when they tried to leave, but the police found no evidence of anyone.

Lee Ann and Felicity looked at one another for a long time as if they were perceiving each other's thoughts.

"What is this spirit trying to tell me? Does she not realize she's passed on?" Lee Ann finally asked.

"I don't know, there are so many questions I have. If she did commit suicide, that could be a traumatic enough event to keep her from being able to move on. There could also be something or someone she's holding onto, but one thing is becoming apparent to me," Felicity shared.

"What's that?"

"This Cassie has attached to you. She is attracted to the light you give off as other spirits have in the past, but she also relates to your anger and your situation. She may even be trying to defend you and keep you from being bullied the way she was. This is a very potentially dangerous situation." Felicity's forehead creased up again with concern.

"So, what do I do?" Lee Ann swallowed hard, not liking what she was hearing, although she had suspected as much herself.

"You have to try and make contact with her. See if you can get her to tell you why she's still there," Felicity suggested.

"But I have tried. When I ask her what she wants, I get silence," Lee Ann recalled.

"You have to go to the waterfall again, the site of her death. She will come to you as she has before."

"But she doesn't really come to me," Lee Ann complained.

"Lee Ann, all of the dreams you 've been having and everything else like waking up on the edge of the cliff were means of communication that she was using."

"Why can't she just speak directly to me and tell me?"

"She was trying, but I can sense that you were trying to block her out," Felicity insisted.

"Well yeah, I would try and put it out of my mind, so I don't flunk anything this semester. It was kind of hard trying to study when you have those sorts of things happening."

"You must open yourself to it, the same way I witnessed you opening yourself that night in the woods two years ago when you released your fear and sadness," Felicity recalled. Lee Ann sighed and let Felicity's words sink in.

"Will you come with me? I need your help if you can," Lee Ann implored, putting her hand on Felicity's.

"Of course I will, my dear." Felicity's calming demeanor and words of reassurance comforted Lee Ann.

CHAPTER

TEN

EMOTIONAL RESCUE

Lee Ann went home, checking her phone on her way back to see if David had ever responded to her. He hadn't, and she was growing increasingly concerned about it. She impulsively decided to stop by his house on the way home, taking a detour down Hamlet Street instead of taking the road out of town once she passed the town square. She saw David's truck sitting in the driveway when she reached his parents' house, about midway down the street. A second after that, her eyes landed on David who was sitting on the front porch swing talking to someone. He hadn't seen her as she was behind the truck where she stopped when she heard the unmistakable, hateful voice of Mary Hartford. Immediately, she turned to head back down the street as tears began to form in her eyes.

"Lee Ann?" David said as he noticed her walking down the street from where he sat.

She hurried her pace, not wanting to face this awkward situation. The twin emotions of sadness and jealousy descended on her as she let her mind speculate about the nature of David and Mary's relationship.

"Wait!" he shouted, but now she was running away.

"What is SHE doing here?" Lee Ann could just make out Mary saying.

David attempted to catch up to Lee Ann but gave up as she got to the main road and kept running.

She stopped and caught her breath when she thought she had put enough distance between her and David's house. The tears came flooding out despite her efforts to stave them off.

How could he be hanging out with her after all we've been through together and the way she treated me!

The anger and sadness she'd been feeling soon turned to guilt as she thought of the late night texts he had sent that she hadn't responded to, being preoccupied with her own circumstances.

This is my fault. I closed myself off to him when he needed me, and he could have helped me. If I hadn't been so closed off and self-absorbed, this wouldn't have happened.

Lee Ann looked at her phone; it was time to meet up with Katrina and Jasmine over at Katrina's house. There was a text from David waiting for her as well. All that it said was

It's not what it looks like, I swear. Please, I want to see you. I know you're upset, but I need you to believe me.

She didn't know what to believe, but she wanted to trust him. Although he sometimes had a hard time keeping secrets, for the most part, he had told her the truth over the course of their relationship. He had stood by her through many tough times and always had her back. Lee Ann dried her eyes, not wanting to look like an emotional train wreck when she saw Jasmine and Katrina. When she reached the small, white stucco cottage that was Katrina's parents' house, she had managed to calm down a bit.

"Everything ok?" Jasmine immediately asked when Katrina opened the front door and they both saw Lee Ann's dejected visage.

"NO!" she said as she hugged them, and another round of tears came pouring out.

Between sobs and deep breaths, Lee Ann unloaded the events of the last few weeks up to when she saw David with Mary. She sat down on the loveseat opposite Jasmine and Katrina who sat down on a large, brown leather couch.

"Well, that's a lot to take in. My God, all I can say is I'm so sorry!" Katrina offered.

"Same here! You deserve so much better than that. Who can blame you if your grades are less than stellar," Jasmine said. Lee Ann took a moment to absorb her friends' appearances. Jasmine had the same sense of style, only now her hair was a blue tint; she had the same colorful braids pulled back into pigtails and a new assemblage of bracelets on her arm. Katrina had lost weight and seemed more confident. Her energy was more relaxed although she was still the same fidgety, quirky girl with glasses.

"Listen, you know we've got your back. We're going to go back with you and be there for you," Katrina reassured her.

"I know you do, but I can't ask you guys to put your lives on hold every time I'm in need of an emotional boost," Lee Ann answered.

"Are you kidding? That's what we're here for. We know you would do the same for us," Jasmine added.

"You guys are the best," she said, reaching over for a group hug. For a moment, she could feel the support needed to face everything just like she felt on that night, two years ago.

"So, what's this about David and Mary?" Katrina asked, always happy to engage in a little gossip.

"I thought maybe you guys might know," Lee Ann stated.

"We haven't really seen him much since graduation," Katrina said.

"Yeah, just around town sometimes," Jasmine added.

"Do you ever see him with her?" Lee Ann inquired.

"No, actually. To tell the truth, I can't see him getting with her. It's not like him," Jasmine pointed out.

"Well, he got with her a long time ago, kissed her one night," Lee Ann recalled.

"I doubt that he would do that again, frankly," Katrina echoed.

"So why was she at his house?" Lee Ann asked no one in particular.

Jasmine and Katrina looked at each other and shrugged their shoulders.

"Beats me. You need to ask him. Allow him to explain himself at least," Katrina suggested.

Lee Ann took out her phone and saw about four messages from David. She opened the last one which said,

Give me a chance to explain, please, Lee Ann.

"Do you mind if I call him really quick?" she asked her friends.

"Sure, go on. It will make you feel better if you do," Jasmine said. Katrina nodded in agreement.

"You guys are the best! I know I said that already," Lee Ann said as she walked into the next room and dialed David's number.

"Hello!" he immediately answered. She could feel the anxiousness in his voice.

"Hey," she answered, simply.

"Let me explain why Mary was at my house, ok?"

"Sure, I'm listening," Lee Ann said, trying not to be sassy.

"She came over with her father to talk about some business. Dad's going to work on Mary's father's next campaign for state representative."

That sounded plausible to Lee Ann because she knew that Mary's family were good friends with David's. Their fathers had been known to play golf together.

"I was just talking to her about you as a matter of fact," he stated.

"Me?"

"Yes, I was defending you when she tried to talk smack."

"What did she say?"

"She tried to say you made up the whole ghost story thing and that you exaggerated the events of that night to get attention," David shared.

"No surprise there- she never believed it. I'm grateful that you did that, and I owe you a huge apology, for not being there for you like I should have been, for all those texts that I didn't answer 'til the next day or at all. I'm just sorry for everything, David. You mean so much to me and I couldn't stand it if you didn't want to talk to me anymore. I need you," she confessed, feeling tears welling up again. It was the most she had cried in years, and she was a bit embarrassed by it.

"It's ok, Lee Ann. All is forgiven. I just can't wait to see you. When can I?"

"I'm over here with Jasmine and Katrina. Do you want to come over and visit with all of us or wait until later so we can be alone?"

"No offense to them, I would love to see them, but I want you all to myself," David confessed.

"No problem. I'll come over tonight, how about six?"

"Perfect!" Lee Ann answered, feeling relief and reassurance washing over her.

"They made up!" Katrina shouted when she saw the smile on Lee Ann's face.

"I knew there was an explanation," Jasmine added.

Later that day, Lee Ann and David took their favorite hike to Widow's Bluff trying to reach the overlook just at the time of sunset. Much to their delight, the sun was spreading its multicolored quilt over the horizon when they reached the top.

"Weird to think we saw a fire the last time we were here," David recalled as he took Lee Ann's hand. They looked over in the direction of Thief's Hollow, and Lee Ann allowed herself to remember the night she discovered her abilities to help others once she could help herself. It gave her strength to face what awaited her back at Farthington.

"Where are you right now?" David asked, waving a hand in front of Lee Ann's face.

"I'm here with you, silly. I was just thinking of that night and how it proves that I can deal with the current drama I'm facing," she said.

"That's right. You're the strongest woman I've ever known!" he pointed out.

She glared at him slightly. "Do you mean I'm strong for a woman?"

"No, no baby. I mean you are strong for a human!" He quickly pointed out.

"That's better!" They sat hand in hand silently for several moments watching the last of the sun's light dissipate over the shadowy hills.

By the time Lee Ann got home, she felt so refreshed and relieved that she'd almost forgotten about the situation that awaited her back at school. She gave a brief greeting to Charles and Shirley, went upstairs, got in bed, and immediately drifted off to sleep.

CHAPTER
ELEVEN
CONTACT

The campus seemed peaceful in the absence of the students. The tree-lined walkways and roads were free of traffic and only the wind made any noise, scraping and rustling the browning leaves against the ground.

"Wow, fancy," David said, looking around at the pink marble buildings and handcrafted wooden doors stolidly standing against the cool breeze.

"Believe me, it's much nicer when the snobby students aren't here," Lee Ann remarked.

"Man, I could see myself reading a novel or twelve under these awesome trees, and this Gothic architecture," Katrina gushed.

"Man, what? This place is incredible," Jasmine echoed. "And you're right in the heart of the mountains; the whole place looks like a state park or something!"

Felicity was quiet. Her eyes were closed as she breathed in the air, trying to get a feel of the energy of the place. She opened her eyes and looked to Lee Ann, then looked off in the direction of the water-fall trail, sensing something.

"Take us to your dorm. I want to see it!" Jasmine implored.

"This way!" Lee Ann answered, pointing down the gravel path. It seemed to her that the presence of her friends had, temporarily at least, banished the negative feelings she had experienced there. The sun shone brightly on a perfect, crisp fall day that seemed to make the recent events unreal, like a bad dream that vanished with the light of dawn.

As they approached the cabin, Felicity's usual peaceful expression began to change.

"What do you sense?" Lee Ann asked her.

"Definitely picking up on her energy, although it seems some distance away. There is such anger and unrest; it's even worse than I suspected, I'm afraid," Felicity shared. The others looked around at each other as if they weren't so sure about the place after all.

As they approached the cabin, Katrina's eyes lit up.

"Wow, it's like you're at summer camp or something. These cabins look like the kind that the CCC built back in the thirties," Katrina stated.

"Only you would know something like that," David teased.

"Well, it certainly hasn't felt like summer camp, I assure you," Lee Ann answered.

Lee Ann unlocked the door, switched on the light, and led them into the empty cabin.

Felicity halted just inside the door, closed her eyes, and breathed deeply the same way she did when they first got there. The place looked cleaner than she had left it, so she guessed that Connor must have cleaned up before she left to go home for the break.

"My roommate, Connor isn't here. She's the one that keeps the place so clean," Lee Ann said.

"There has been something here, but it feels different," Felicity revealed.

"Well, Cassie has visited me here I'm pretty sure," Lee Ann pointed out.

"It's not her," Felicity answered.

"Hmmm, then who is it? Lee Ann inquired.

"Not completely sure, but it feels like a female energy, a kind, but solemn energy- very different from Cassie's."

"Maybe it's the other girl, Katie," David reasoned.

"Good guess, David," Felicity answered.

"Maybe she's nearby too, but I've never sensed her," Lee Ann indicated.

"So, what's the game plan for making contact with this Cassie?" Katrina asked.

"We need to go to the site of her death: the waterfall overlook. We need to go at the time of day when Lee Ann has had her experiences, at twilight just before dark," Felicity suggested.

"I don't know how I didn't think to do that before," Lee Ann remarked as she shook her head thinking back to the woman that would always appear at the same time each night during the Thief's Hollow incident.

In the meantime, they cooked burgers on the grill behind the cabin as the afternoon wore on. They all sat around the grill in folded chairs that Felicity had brought for just such an occasion watching David flip the burgers.

"This takes me back to that night at Thief's Hollow when we camped out there," David recalled.

"Yeah, what a crazy time," Jasmine stated.

"I just wish I could have all of you here and it not be a crazy time. I've roped you guys into another situation," Lee Ann moaned, shaking her head.

"Hey, that's what we're here for," Katrina said, smacking her knee lightly.

"Yeah," David agreed, putting his arm around her.

"Seriously, you guys make me feel like I could ban the bell witch and chase off the jersey devil," Lee Ann joked. Felicity smiled at this, knowing that their support was already having a positive effect on Lee Ann.

"You don't have to feel that way. As you yourself once said, you didn't ask for this. You have a special gift, and no matter where you try and go and how hard you try and resist, you will still be contact-ed," Felicity insisted. This seemed to depress Lee Ann, causing her to hang her head.

"But it is a gift, Lee Ann, not a curse! You are allowed a glimpse into a world that others only guess at or dismiss as unreal. The help you can provide is so necessary for those who can't transition. Without people like you, we would have so many souls aimlessly repeating tragic moments, unable to let go of their lives as they most certainly must. And the more you resist your gifts, the more they will strive for your attention," Felicity suggested. She put her hand on Lee Ann's and smiled. Lee Ann knew deep down that Felicity was right.

After they finished eating, the sun was almost at the horizon, signaling the oncoming evening.

"Take us to the waterfall's edge," Felicity said, turning to Lee Ann.

They followed Lee Ann in single file to the trailhead. They could hear the whisper of nearby waters punctuated by the occasional stir-ring in the underbrush or birdsong.

"I would normally be really stoked about a hike like this, but what you've told us puts a damper on things," David shared. Katrina and Jasmine looked at each other and nodded in agreement.

Lee Ann took David's hand and smiled at him.

"Having all of you here makes this place feel a heck of a lot less creepy, I assure you," Lee Ann said.

Felicity pulled her shawl around herself, feeling a slight chill in the air as the trail emptied onto the overlook above the waterfall. The closeness of the forest gave way to flat, gray rock split apart by the flow of the small but determined stream that ended abruptly at the cliff's edge. The group stopped to take in the breathtaking scenery. Miles of undulating ridges with flat tops common in the Cumberland region stretched out before them decked out in all the colors of fall.

"Wow! How high up do you think we are?" David asked no one in particular.

"I read that the waterfall is about seventy-five feet high," Lee Ann announced,

David stepped closer to the edge, looking down. The gushing water crashed into a shallow, boulder-filled pool below.

"Don't get too close to the edge!" Lee Ann insisted.

"What? I'm ok," David answered.

Felicity was focused away from the edge of the cliff towards the woods where they had emerged a moment ago from the trail. She could feel the chill in the air increasing. Lee Ann too could sense something approaching. As twilight bathed the hills, an orb appeared below the tree line. Everyone could see the eerie blue light emitted but only Lee Ann could see the outline of the figure of a girl as the orb moved towards the ground. Felicity took a step backward, feeling increasingly uneasy due to the energy she was picking up on. The hostility, rage and melancholy overwhelmed her, and she began to cry. Everyone suddenly focused their attention on Felicity who suddenly spoke,

"Step back all of you, there is such tremendous rage here," she warned. Even David who wasn't quick to retreat in such instances obeyed her, sensing the urgency. Lee Ann stood her ground and faced the apparition knowing that fear would block her abilities. As the figure drew closer, it materialized for Lee Ann. Although the girl was transparent, Lee Ann could now see the girl had long, curly dark hair and dark eyes with concentric rings beneath them making her look older. She wore a ripped and tattered t-shirt and shorts that were also torn and scratched.

The girl stopped within a couple feet of Lee Ann.

"Who are you and why can you not find peace?" Lee Ann said bluntly. The others were amazed at her courage. They all stood nearby, just behind Felicity. Although no one else could see the girl, they could all sense that something was there.

"My name is Cassie, but you probably have guessed that already. You're smart like me," the voice echoed and reverberated as if they were standing in a room devoid of carpet or furniture. Cassie walked around in a semi-circle as if she were in no hurry. Her eyes glinted with grief mixed with mischief.

"Thank you, I'm Lee Ann, but I suppose you know that already," Lee Ann answered, making Cassie smile. "Can you tell us the answer to the second part of my question?" Lee Ann insisted.

"You like to cut to the chase, I like that. Again, so much like me," Cassie continued.

By now, the materialization was so strong, the entire assembled group could hear Cassie's voice as it cascaded and echoed like waters off the boulders beneath them.

"Lee Ann, I know that you know how it feels when everything you say or wear or do is judged by others. I know that you know the torture of going through your day and not knowing when other girls are going to terrorize you, make fun of you for wearing black eyeliner or listening to the Sex Pistols or thinking that their boyfriends are looking at you."

"Yes, I do know what that's like, but you don't have to worry about that now," Lee Ann reassured her.

Cassie giggled at this and shook her head.

"That's all I have to worry about," Cassie said, moving a bit closer.

"You have to let go of all of that," Lee Ann insisted.

"What about you, Lee Ann? Can you let go? When those girls come back from break, they aren't going to let anything go, are they?"

"I can handle them," Lee Ann said.

Cassie laughed again and shook her head once more, "There will be no peace until all women like Gina stop harassing women like you."

"Please let me help you. I just want to help you to move on," Lee Ann offered.

Cassie turned away for a moment and began a slow, but steady giggle that turned into a full-throated laugh. It sounded both maniacal and morose.

"I can't move on. I can't because of Samantha," Cassie answered. She turned back towards Lee Ann revealing an angry scowl which faded into shadow illuminated only by Cassie's glowing red eyes. The laughing became more of a cackling.

"Move back further!" Felicity warned the others as Lee Ann took a step to the side to put some distance between her and Cassie.

The shadow-like figure moved into the air with one swooping motion and emerged at the waterfall's edge as a glowing orb again. It tumbled into the waters below and disappeared.

Lee Ann went over to join the others hugging David who held her tightly to him.

"It's ok, it's over," Felicity said.

They were all shook up that night and it took a while for everyone to settle in. Felicity sat with Lee Ann on the couch while the others slept.

"What do we need to do now?" Lee Ann asked bluntly.

"Well, Cassie revealed a couple of important things to us and for that we are fortunate. On the other hand, I don't' think I've ever dealt with such an enraged and unsettled energy. She is quite volatile, and we must use great care. I fear that there is the potential for great danger, especially when it comes to encounters with Gina and her friends.

"What's to be done?"

"If there is some way to find a resolution to the bullying, a way to get Gina to stop, that could appease her," Felicity suggested.

Lee Ann laughed and put her head back, "I don't think there's any way to get her to do that. She hates me too much," Lee Ann insisted.

"Well, we must try. As I stated before, I believe that the bullying has attracted Cassie and that perhaps she will not stop her manifestations until the behavior stops. The other piece of information that Cassie shared is this Samantha person. We need to probe further into the story and find out exactly what happened that night and find out just who this Samantha is. I have a hunch that she was Cassie's tormentor the same as Gina is yours."

"Let's not go that far; I feel like it makes Gina seem a lot tougher than she is. Seriously though, I had a hunch already that we didn't have the full story," Lee Ann agreed.

"We need to talk to anyone we can that might know more about what happened to Cassie," Felicity stated. Lee Ann nodded in agreement.

CHAPTER
TWELVE
ENIGMA

As the break wound to a close, Lee Ann's friends had to return home to see to various obligations. Felicity had a business to run, and there was no one available if she wanted to take off. She would simply have to close for that day and lose potential income. David, Jasmine, and Katrina all had jobs they had to return to. Lee Ann felt completely isolated as she walked away from the parking lot where she watched Felicity and the others drive off in her green sedan. The vision of David turned around in the back seat blowing her a kiss was too much for her and she began to cry as she made her way down the path towards her cabin.

Its ok, we can face this, she assured herself, taking deep breaths to gather strength from deep within her. She was most pleased to see the light on in the cabin and the familiar sight of Connor's legs over her top bunk.

"Hey! How'd your visit go?" Lee Ann asked, feeling immediately relieved to be in the presence of another human being.

"Oh fine, not really eventful enough to talk about," Connor replied in a somewhat hushed voice. "How about you?"

"It went great for the most part, and we've made some progress on the Cassie front," Lee Ann revealed, moving in closer as her excitement grew.

"We made contact with Cassie, and she told us that she couldn't be at rest because of Samantha," Lee Ann went on. Connor's eyes lit up a bit.

"So, you must find out who she is and what her connection to Cassie's death is," Connor responded.

"Exactly. What's puzzling is why Cassie hasn't come right out and told me this sooner."

"Maybe she's been trying, but you've been blocking her out," Connor suggested.

"Yeah, that's what Felicity said too. I just don't know how I can be expected to juggle all this coursework while I try to solve this puzzle," Lee Ann bemoaned as she sat down on her bed and buried her head in her hands.

"Hey look, we'll figure this out together, don't worry," Connor said as if she already knew that everything would resolve itself.

"I wish I felt as confident as you, but I have to find a way to appease Cassie so I can get on with my own life. I'm going to try and reason with Gina and get her to just leave me alone. Felicity has a theory that Cassie has attached herself to me because I'm like her in many ways, and I'm going through the same experiences she went through. Felicity thinks that if I can get the harassment to stop, it may put Cassie at ease."

"Hmm, but will that be enough to appease her? What if what she wants is justice?" Connor suggested.

"Do you think that this Samantha person caused her to commit suicide because of her harassment?" Lee Ann asked.

"Hmm, maybe. What if it isn't suicide at all?" Connor reasoned.

"We need to try and talk to people who knew Cassie or anyone that can give us information about what happened that day, and we've got to find this Samantha," Lee Ann stated. Connor nodded and smiled.

Later that afternoon after her classes, Lee Ann sat sketching the edge of the forest near the trailhead for Whispering Falls. Her thoughts wandered far and wide pondering the possibilities with the Cassie situation. The burden lay heavy on her as she thought about the assignments that she needed to be working on but was putting off due to emotional fatigue.

I'll get to those tonight after I have a chance to clear my head.

As she continued to sketch, she began to hear footsteps coming from the winding path that led from Whitten Hall to the trailhead. She turned to see Derrick making his way down the path. He smiled and waved at her. She waved back at him.

"What are you sketching?" he asked, stopping near her.

"Oh, just trees and such. I'm trying to put off doing my class-work," Lee Ann answered.

"Me too. I think it's cool how you're an artist and all," he said, smiling again. Lee Ann could feel his attraction toward her, and it made her feel a bit awkward.

"Eh, I wouldn't' really call myself an artist as such, maybe an artist in training. I'll get there," Lee Ann said with a half-smile.

"I actually took an art history course last semester," Derrick shared.

'Oh? That's cool. Did you like it?" Lee Ann answered, looking around to make sure that Gina wasn't hiding in a bush somewhere watching them.

"It was really interesting! I wish I had more time to take elective courses, but the pressure's on to finish on time," He shared.

"What's your major? Sorry, I know it's a lame question that everyone gets asked," Lee Ann inquired.

"Business," he said succinctly.

"Ah," Lee Ann said, thinking how typical that was.

"But I want to start a non-profit," he said, sensing that Lee Ann wasn't impressed.

"That's cool," Lee Ann said, wanting to end the conversation.

Just then, Lee Ann's eye caught a glimpse of Gina down the path the same way Derrick had come. Although it was too far for her to tell for sure, it seemed to Lee Ann that Gina was scowling.

"Ugh, your girlfriend is coming," Lee Ann said. Derrick turned and waved to Gina who did not wave back.

"See you around," Derrick said to Lee Ann and proceeded to walk towards Gina.

"What are you doing?" Lee Ann could overhear Gina saying. The rest of their argument was harder to make out.

"Gina, don't...." Derrick said a moment later as Gina pulled away from him and walked towards Lee Ann.

"I swear to God...." Gina said as she drew closer to Lee Ann who got to her feet to face her.

"Gina, just relax," Lee Ann said, trying to remain as level-headed as possible.

"Don't tell me to relax when every time I turn around, you're talking to my boyfriend!" Gina snapped taking a large step closer to Lee Ann.

"He came up to me, just like before," Lee Ann insisted.

Gina paused as Derrick appeared behind her.

"That's true, Gina," he confessed.

"What the hell, Derrick? Are you interested in her now?" Gina turned to face him.

"No, I'm just being nice to her. You should try it some time. People respond well to it," he said angrily before turning to walk away.

Gina was about to follow him, but her rage overwhelmed her. She pushed Lee Ann and yelled at her.

"The next time I see you near my boyfriend, you are going to regret it!" Just then, Gina suddenly lost her footing as if she slipped or some unseen force pushed her over. She fell onto her behind, bracing herself with her palms outward. Her mouth fell open in disbelief because this time, she could clearly tell that Lee Ann hadn't pushed her.

"What the?" Gina stammered unsure how to respond.

"You see, Gina you must stop what you're doing. That girl, Cassie, the one who died at the falls years and years ago. She is the one pushing you. She wants you to stop the way you're treating me. It's likely that she was treated the same way years ago and she identifies with me because of that."

"What? You expect me to believe that?" Gina sneered as she got to her feet.

"Look, I know it's hard to except, but there is something paranormal going on here."

"I guess you would know, ghost girl," Gina hissed. "I'm not afraid of whatever is going on and I'm certainly not afraid of you, Lee Ann. So, if you are asking me to just start being nice to you in the hopes that this thing will stop happening, forget it! This isn't over!" Gina scowled before turning to walk away.

Lee Ann, realizing how behind she was in two of her classes, returned to the cabin to catch up on her reading. She took a deep breath and began to read over her Art History textbook. Ordinarily, she would have been excited to read just about anything on this subject, but this day she read the same paragraph three times and realized that she still had no idea what she just read.

Maybe I need something to eat, she thought to herself after about half an hour.

"Hey, I'm going to the cafeteria to grab a bite, wanna come or want me to bring you back something?" she asked Connor, who was tapping her foot along to the music coming through her headphone where she lay in her bunk.

"No thanks, I'm good," She responded.

Lee Ann made her way to the cafeteria, hoping not to have any encounters with Gina or her friends. Just as she was about to walk into the entrance, a voice ushered from above her head.

"Hey Lee Ann!" Gina called out. Lee Ann looked up, just as Gina and Claire lowered a huge homer bucket full of leftover cafeteria food and drink that immediately found its mark and covered her head, spilling onto her shoulders and shirt.

Lee Ann stood there stunned for a moment while several people laughed at the sight of her, none more than Gina and Claire. Derrick was there with two of his friends; he looked up at Gina and shook his head disapprovingly although he didn't speak up to offer his opinions.

"Still hungry?" Gina mocked. Lee Ann scowled at her and immediately ran around the side of the building, looking for a way to get to the roof. She was so angry she wasn't sure what she would do if she caught up to them. Gina and Claire made their way to the ladder on the east side of the building as Lee Ann made her way up from a fire escape stairwell on the west side of the building. By the time she reached the top, they were already on the ground and running away, laughing amongst themselves. She climbed down as her tormentors ran off towards the dorms.

The students in the area were either laughing or staring up at Lee Ann in astonishment. Julie happened to be there, and she immediately ran up to Lee Ann to offer her sympathies.

"I saw the whole thing. So horrible. I am so sorry, Lee Ann. I will report this to security," Julie stated.

"Thanks Julie, I really appreciate that," Lee Ann responded.

"I'm scheduled to give a tour in a few minutes, so I have to run but I promise you that this isn't over," Julie assured her.

"You're the best. Thanks!" Lee Ann said, waving to her as she drove off in the golf cart.

Derrick ran to get a towel from inside the cafeteria and came running up to give it to Lee Ann. His anger with Gina was such that he didn't care who witnessed his kindness towards Lee Ann.

"Here," he said, extending the towel towards her. She took it and began to wipe the food from her hair and face. She smelled of old meat and an array of sauces that had never meant to be mixed.

"I am so sorry that she did that to you. I want you to know I fully intend to break up with her after that," he declared.

"Thank you," Lee Ann acknowledged as tears began to well up in her eyes. Finally, the dam burst; not knowing who else to turn to she fell into Derrick's arms and let him hug and comfort her.

"Lee Ann, you deserve so much better than this. You are smart, beautiful, and really cool...." She could feel his desire moving through him as he hugged her tighter. She pulled away slowly.

"Thank you for being so kind...." She turned away from him and walked quickly away. Derrick thought about going after her, but he began to realize he may have gone too far. Becky had been standing by and saw the whole thing. Her expression looked a bit perplexed like she was struggling to find her thoughts on the situation.

Lee Ann decided to immediately go to the Dean's office to file a harassment complaint and possibly try and get a restraining order against Gina and Claire or at least some protection from campus security. It was not her normal way as she would ordinarily try to settle things on her own, but that had clearly gotten her nowhere. She waited in the lobby of the Dean's office for half an hour before she was able to get in. Other people waiting there gave her strange looks due to the huge grease stains all over her shirt and pants and the smell of old food that radiated from her. The Dean was a tall, short-haired woman with large, brown eyes with a look that seemed to convey both concern and smugness to Lee Ann. Her name was Linda Barton, and it had taken her twenty years to move up through the ranks to her current position.

Lee Ann explained the whole ongoing situation between her and Gina, being careful to leave out the parts that she knew they would question, meaning anything that had to do with Cassie. The Dean listened to her words very carefully as she laced her hands together. Finally, she put one hand up to her chin as if deep in thought. She nodded here or there, but for the most part didn't speak until Lee Ann was finished with her account.

"I see. This is most unfortunate to hear, and first, let me just say that this sort of behavior is never tolerated here at Farthington. I will investigate the matter immediately, and Gina Haskell will be in hot water if she threatens or intimidates you again. We want nothing more than for you to have the most fulfilling experience and education you can possibly have," she declared. Lee Ann nodded, sensing that she was hearing some sort of rehearsed response. Before she could utter a reply, the Dean's phone rang.

"One second," The Dean said, picking up the phone. "Yes? Oh, alright, send him in..."

"The headmaster wishes to speak with you for a moment," The Dean said.

"Oh, eh, ok," Lee Ann responded, not sure what to make of this.

Ronald Blevins had been the Headmaster of Farthington since the early seventies. Although many had encouraged him to consider retiring now that he was eighty years old, he seemed determined to remain Headmaster for as long as he possibly could.

"Hello, Lee Ann, I'm Headmaster Blevins. Your situation has come to my attention, and I wanted to extend my sympathies and sincerest apologies for your treatment here at Farthington. I understand that you've suffered some harassment and bullying and those are things we don't tolerate here. I assure you all of this will come to a stop!"

"Thank you, sir, I really appreciate your concern," she replied.

"There's something else. I have also heard rumors of Gina being visited in the night, and some other strange goings on...."

Lee Ann fidgeted a bit in her seat, unsure of how to respond to this.

"Yes, I've heard about that as well," Lee Ann finally acknowledged.

"Now, this wouldn't be some attempt at revenge on your part, to give her a good scare capitalizing on some old legend, would it?" he asked, cocking an eyebrow as his and the Dean's eyes bore down on her.

"No sir! I wouldn't dare do such a thing. All I want is to be left alone, I swear," Lee Ann declared. The Dean and Headmaster both looked at her intently for a moment before the headmaster spoke up again,

"Well, good. Let's just make sure we don't have any more of these incidents. We wouldn't want the whole college to be frightened of their own shadows now, do we?"

"Of course not," Lee Ann answered.

"Good. I think we understand each other, Lee Ann. You are quite a smart and talented girl, and I am very impressed with the credentials you came with. However, I do see that you've had some struggles with your grades, and I would like to see you refocus your attention on those pursuits. I would hate to see you waste too much time chasing old stories that will lead you nowhere. I know a case of female infighting when I see one, and I understand there is a boy involved as well…"

"But I have a boyfriend and have no interest in Derrick whatsoever…." Lee Ann snapped back, clinching her fists in a more defensive posture.

"Well now, that's good to hear. Please do let us know if Gina or her friends give you any more trouble, and don't take the law into your own hands. Very nice chatting with you, Lee Ann," the headmaster said, giving her a smile she thought a car salesman might give.

What the hell was that all about? Lee Ann asked herself as she exited the building and made her way back to the dorms.

When Lee Ann got back to the cabin, she told Connor about the encounter with the headmaster. Connor sat with her legs dangling over her bed in the usual manner, listening intently to every word.

"I think the headmaster wants to keep everyone from panicking, I get that, but something about the way he said, 'I don't want you chasing down stories that will lead you nowhere' was really odd," Lee Ann opined.

"Yeah, that almost sounds threatening like he doesn't want you to try and find out what happened, like he has something to hide," Connor mused.

"Yes, exactly! That just makes me want to get to the bottom of things even more. I need to find out who this Samantha is and see if I can even get in touch with her or at the very least, find out what her connection to Cassie is. I also have to find a way to convince Gina to stop how's she treating me. I'm afraid of what Cassie will do. I just wish I knew how to make it all stop."

"Sounds like you are asking all the right questions. Once you know what actually happened and have proof of it, you can put the matter to rest," Connor replied, sounding very assured.

"You make it sound so straight forward, but that seems so hard right now considering how much Gina hates me," Lee Ann sighed. They both decided that they would do some digging the next day to figure out who Samantha was and even try and contact her.

Lee Ann finally drifted off into an uneasy sleep. She dreamed of walking through the moonlit campus towards Gina's cabin.

CHAPTER

THIRTEEN

RETALIATION

Gina and her friends laughed about the day's events while Becky sat off in the corner by herself painting her toenails.

"The look on her stupid face..." Gina went on.

"I know, it was precious," Claire added as they laughed together.

"What's the matter, Becky? Did we mess up your friend's day?"

"She's not my friend. I just don't understand why you won't leave her alone," Becky said, turning to face them.

"Well, I wonder how you would feel if Lee Ann were talking to Steve all the time," Gina stated, putting her hands on her hips.

"Derrick is always trying to talk to her," Becky insisted.

Gina glared at her, throwing a shoe across the room that missed Becky by a foot or so.

"No, that's just not true!" Gina barked.

"I'm afraid it is, and I think you've taken things too far. Why do you think we got called into the Dean's office today?"

"She didn't even threaten us, she just wants us to cool it, that's all. After the contributions my family has given this school, they aren't about to do a single thing, I assure you," Gina scoffed. Their conversation was interrupted by Derrick knocking on the door.

LEE ANN HAD a big test coming up the next day, but all she could do was wonder about how to stop the madness that had been taking place as of late. She was torn between trying to find out who Samantha was and trying to get more answers from Cassie about how to appease her and help her to find peace. After about an hour of struggling to concentrate, she finally decided to go to the waterfall and see if she could get more answers. Cassie declined the invitation to go with her.

The afternoon was cloudy and cool, interspersed with bursts of wind that sent leaves flying in circular whorls across the fields. Lee Ann made her way towards the trailhead as groups of students passed her going both directions. A familiar face soon appeared beside her.

"Hey, we meet again," said Derrick who smiled at her.

"Look, you are a nice guy, but I think I need to clarify some things. I have a boyfriend, you have a girlfriend, and that particular girlfriend wants to kill me because she hates it when you talk to me," Lee Ann pointed out. Derrick did not stop smiling at her.

"Well, you are partly correct. I actually don't have a girlfriend anymore. I broke up with Gina just a few minutes ago," he proudly stated.

"What? You did what?" Lee Ann was in shock.

"Yeah, I don't want to be with someone who treats people the way she treated you," Derrick said.

"Well, I can understand that, but you need to understand, and don't take this the wrong way because you seem like a nice guy and all, but I'm not interested in you...like that." She chose her words carefully so as not to insult or upset him.

"I know, I just want to be your friend, that's all," he stated matter-of-factly.

94

"Oh, well I suppose that's ok," she conceded.

'Where are you headed?" he asked.

"I was about to try and talk to a ghost," she revealed.

"Oh, you mean the one that keeps messing with Gina. I think they call her Cassie, don't they?" Derrick stated.

"Yeah, that's the one."

"You mind if I tag along?" Lee Ann paused for a moment, unsure of what to do. The truth was she welcomed the company but didn't want to lead him on.

"Eh, sure, why not?" she answered after a moment.

Before long, they reached the overlook. For a moment, Lee Ann became lost in the view in front of them. The distant hills spread out like an endless blanket of vibrant leaves mixed with bare patches where the trees had already lost theirs. The sun was sitting low in the sky, spreading out a mosaic of color like buckets of paint had been spilled just over the horizon.

"That's really something, isn't it?" Derrick remarked.

"Yeah, for a moment I forgot how messed up things are." She took out her phone to check the time and saw that twilight was just a few moments away.

"So how does this work, talking to ghosts and such?" he finally asked.

"Well, nothing special really. Most people can't actually see a disembodied spirit. I unfortunately have the ability, and they always want to come to me because they sense that I can help them."

Derrick nodded his head, but he wasn't entirely sure what to make of all of this.

As the light began to fade around them, Lee Ann decided the time was right.

"I'm going to try and make contact with her," she told Derrick who stood about two yards to her right.

"Cassie, are you here? Will you come and speak with me?"

The wind rustled in the trees, but no voice was heard. Instead, the two of them could make out the sound of someone walking hurriedly up the trail just behind them.

"Is that her coming up the trail?" Derrick asked, his eyes wide with anticipation that he might really witness some sort of supernatural event.

"I don't know," Lee Ann said as the sound of footsteps through the leaves grew louder.

Lee Ann was quite surprised to see Gina standing about ten feet away from them. Her face was smeared with running makeup and tears.

"I knew it! You broke up with me for this TRASH!" she said in a fit of rage, taking a step forward.

"No, Gina. It's not at all what it looks like," Lee Ann insisted.

"You! Why the hell would I believe anything you have to say, ghost girl? You've obviously had designs on my man all this time. Well, I guess you got what you wanted!" She took another two steps in their direction while Derrick moved closer to her.

"Gina, Lee Ann is right. There is nothing going on between the two of us. I just happened to be walking by the area and just wanted to help her."

"What BS! Can't you even admit that you like her?" Gina began sobbing as her anger grew. Derrick moved closer, fearing that she might try and hurt Lee Ann.

Lee Ann looked behind her and realized that she was only two steps away from the edge of the cliff. She examined her options, which were few.

"I have had it with you!" Gina yelled as she rushed forward towards Lee Ann who took a step back and slipped on the loose rock. She lost her footing, fell on her chest and her legs were now dangling over the cliff. Gina moved forward again and was only a few feet away from Lee Ann. Derrick grabbed Lee Ann's left hand and began to pull her to safety as Gina grew closer. Suddenly, Gina flew backwards and landed on her behind, her palms were planted flat to brace herself.

A shadowy figure appeared between Gina and Lee Ann who was now on her feet thanks to Derrick's assistance.

"I told you to leave her alone!" a strange voice hissed from overhead. Gina, Derrick, and Lee Ann all looked up at the space above them although only Lee Ann could see the transparent figure of Cassie floating there, her eyes glowing hot like angry embers.

"No, don't hurt her!" Lee Ann exclaimed as Cassie turned towards her.

Cassie's eyes changed color and her expression softened. She vanished into the air as quickly as she appeared.

"Wait, I have questions! I want to help you!" Lee Ann called out, but there was no response.

Gina broke out into a fit of sobs. Derrick, feeling bad for her ran over to her and helped her get to her feet.

"Are you ok?" Derrick asked Lee Ann.

"I'm fine. Thanks for helping me up," she said.

Gina ran off down the trail filling the woods with the sound of her sobs.

"I better go check on her," he said to Lee Ann who nodded in agreement. Lee Ann stuck around for several more minutes as the darkness gathered around her, trying to get Cassie to communicate with her to no avail.

ABOUT AN HOUR LATER, Derrick kissed Gina goodnight in front of her cabin.

"Are you sure you are going to be alright?" Derrick asked her.

"Yes, I'm fine," she said, still angry that she caught him alone with Lee Ann.

"Whoa, what the hell happened?" Claire asked. Gina told them the whole story.

"So, a ghost pushed you to the ground?" Becky asked.

"I don't know what happened. I may have slipped. All I know is that this is not over. Who does Lee Ann think she is sneaking around with other people's boyfriends?"

"Well, technically he wasn't your boyfriend at that moment," Becky pointed out.

"Well, we just got back together so he is now. Besides, whose side are you on? She is going to pay for trying to steal him away from me!"

"You have got to leave Lee Ann alone, don't you see?" Becky implored.

"Cassie is trying to protect her, and she is going to end up hurting you if you don't stop!" Becky went on. Claire didn't comment, but she nodded in agreement.

"Look, I don't claim to know exactly what's going on here, but one thing's for sure. No freak girl is going to try and steal my man away and get away with it!" she declared.

Soon, they all grew tired and fell asleep one by one as silence fell upon the campus. The clouds interspersed moonlight and shadow on the quads and buildings as a restless wind blew around Gina, Claire, and Becky's cabin.

A sound that could have been an owl came from the woods nearby. Becky awoke first, hearing the sound which was somewhere between a hoot and a cackle. She heard it again, closer this time. It sounded disturbingly and unmistakably human. She got up and walked across the dark room towards the others' beds and stopped at Gina's bedside. Becky looked down in astonishment at Gina whose eyes were wide open, tearing up with fear, her mouth trembling and agape.

"I cccccan't move," Gina whimpered. Something is holding me down..." Becky put her hand up to her mouth as she heard the strange cackle again. This time she could tell it was coming from inside the room with them. She finally got herself together enough to put her hand in Gina's and attempt to pull her up. After several efforts, Becky managed to help her to her feet.

"I've got to get out of here, Becky!" Gina declared. Becky had never seen so much fear in Gina's eyes before. Gina was usually the least afraid among them.

Becky helped Gina to get dressed as Claire began to stir.

"What's going on guys?" Claire moaned.

"Something's here with us," Becky whispered as if she was afraid whatever it was would hear her. The once stagnant air began to move and chill the room, causing goose bumps to appear on the girls' arms.

Gina put her hand on the doorknob, but it would not turn. Something flung her suddenly against the wall as the large farm table in the center of the room was pushed by unseen forces against the door making their escape impossible. Gina was pinned, struggling to free herself. The others began to feel a sense of panic as they cried out to her.

"Gina!" Claire cried as the cackle issued for the form the space above their heads. A moment later a shadow began to take shape at the far end of the room as if the darkness was concentrating and amassing itself into one space.

The shadow began to resemble the silhouette of a girl with unseen features other than blazing red eyes that shown forth with a rage that filled the three girls with trepidation.

"I told you to leave her alone!" the raspy, echoey voice declared above their heads. Gina slowly began to move up the wall, unable to free herself or move her limbs.

"I thought I told you not to harm her or bother her ever AGAIN!" the voice shrieked as Gina fell to the ground as if the force that held her had suddenly let go of her. The three friends screamed and ran outside, running madly across the moonlit field, waking everyone in the neighboring cabins.

CHAPTER
FOURTEEN
RECONCILIATION

Lee Ann and Connor walked out of the cabin as the flashing lights and howling siren of a police car tore open the night. They had been awoken by Gina, Claire, and Becky's screams.

"Cassie," Lee Ann said to no one in particular.

They sat on the front patio and watched Gina attempt to compose herself, enough to recall what had happened. Her teeth were chattering, her face was pale, and her eyes were wide with a terror that Lee Ann had never witnessed before. For the first time, she felt empathy for her tormentor. She wanted to go to her, but she waited until the questioning was done.

"I feel bad for her. I never wanted her to be terrorized this way," she said to Connor. There was no response from her.

"Connor?" Lee Ann called out, but she wasn't anywhere to be found. Lee Ann figured she must have wanted to get away from the scene, being shy and easily overstimulated.

Once the police were finished talking to Gina and her friends, they walked over to Lee Ann and Connor's cabin. Lee Ann swallowed hard, preparing herself to talk to them.

"Ms. Daniels, just about forty minutes ago, three young ladies were attacked by a woman inside of their cabin just over there," he gestured towards the direction of their cabin. "We just want to ask you a few questions because one of the young ladies said that you and Ms. Haskell have a history of not getting along."

"Well, it's more a case of her bullying me and me trying to defend myself," Lee Ann clarified.

"What were your whereabouts over the last hour or so, Ms. Daniels?"

"I was asleep in my bed. The sound of the screaming woke me up," Lee Ann confirmed.

"Can anyone back up your story?" the other officer asked.

"Yes, my roommate Connor," she answered.

"Where is she?" the other asked.

"I don't know. She's really shy, so she left the scene," Lee Ann shrugged.

The two officers looked at one another.

"Now, if you think she did this, I can assure you that Connor would never..." Lee Ann went on.

"We would like to ask her a few questions..." the taller officer said.

"Sure," Lee Ann conceded as they followed her into the cabin. Lee Ann switched on the light and looked everywhere, but she was nowhere to be found.

"Any idea where she might go?" the shorter one inquired.

"She likes to go hike the waterfall trail," Lee Ann pointed out. The officers looked less than thrilled with the prospect of going down some trail in the dead of a cold night. They walked out of the cabin as Gina approached them.

"It wasn't Lee Ann or anyone that is living, like I told you," Gina exclaimed, in a higher pitched, panicked tone that Lee Ann had never heard before. The officers seemed puzzled as to what to do next. It was obvious that they had never dealt with a situation quite like this before. They filed a report and made arrangements with campus security for someone to patrol the area for the remainder of the evening.

"Would you guys like to stay in our cabin tonight?" Lee Ann asked Gina and her friends. It was a strange turn of events, but eventually they all agreed to her proposal. Lee Ann moved to the couch and offered up her bunk to Gina. Claire set up in the bunk above her while Becky tried to get comfortable in the bed beneath Connor's. Connor was nowhere to be found. Lee Ann began to worry about her and thought about going out to search for her, but she felt deep down that Connor was fine and would come back when she was ready.

"Look, this isn't easy for me to say, but I'm sorry for how I've treated you. I know now for sure that you weren't trying to scare me to get back at me. I also know that you're not interested in Derrick. I know that he was the one being friendly to you, and he and I are still going to have to work through that," she stated.

"It's ok," Lee Ann said with a smile. "I'm just glad that no one was hurt," Lee Ann said.

"Is it over, I mean the whole Cassie thing?" Becky asked Lee Ann.

Lee Ann hesitated for a moment and searched her thoughts.

"I hope so," she finally answered.

The next day was so bright and sunny it was hard to believe it was the same place where the previous events had taken place. It was a Saturday, so no one had to face classes after the turmoil of the night before. Lee Ann showered and got dressed as one by one the other girls woke up. The dean knocked on the door, waking Claire who was the last one still sleeping.

"Girls, if you are ready, I'd like to talk with you," the Dean declared.

The dean sat in the one reclining chair.

"We have another cabin for you girls in the east quad. It is ready for you now. I wanted to follow up with you about last night's events. The local papers and news outlets are asking lots of questions and rumors are spreading about ghosts or prowlers in the area. We want to do our best to settle the fears of locals and get this behind us."

The dean's tone sounded a bit offensive to Lee Ann. It was as if she were only concerned about the P.R. aspect of what had happened and not their well-being.

"Don't you want to know if we're alright?" Lee Ann asked indignantly.

"Of course I do, Lee Ann. I read the police report and I'm aware that no one was hurt."

"Maybe not physically, but this whole thing has been traumatic for everyone involved," Lee Ann insisted.

"I can see that, but we mustn't let our emotions get the better of us, Ms. Daniels. I have a job to do and that's to keep the reputation of Farthington intact. Do you think it's going to attract students if they think there is haunting taking place?" the dean asked.

Lee Ann sighed and flared her nostrils.

"Lee Ann's right. Why aren't you more concerned about us?" Gina chimed in.

"I will make sure that each of you is visited by the staff counselor. In the meantime, I need some assurance from each of you. If you are approached by reporters when you are off campus, I would ask that you decline to speak with them. We are going to put out an official statement and try our best to put the whole thing to rest," the dean declared.

"What is the statement?" Lee Ann inquired.

"That you and Gina were in conflict, and it went too far. We took the proper disciplinary action, and it is now resolved." Lee Ann and Gina looked at each other and then back at the dean.

"Are you going to discipline us?" Becky asked.

"No, but it must look as if we took some action. So, are we in agreement to steer clear of the press?" the dean pressed.

"Ok, I guess so," Lee Ann declared reluctantly. One by one the others agreed. Something didn't settle right with her about the whole situation, but in the end, she didn't want to anger the dean.

Gina and the others left to go move into their new cabin while Lee Ann grabbed her books and went off towards the woods to try and get some work done. For the first time in ages, she was able to focus and read her assignments. After a couple of hours, her thoughts turned to David, Felicity, and the others. She group-texted them, telling them all about the previous night. Then, she talked with David on the phone for over an hour. Everyone seemed relieved that things had been resolved.

By the time she returned to the cabin, Connor was back in her usual spot again waving to her.

"Where did you get off to last night?" Lee Ann asked her.

"I went and stayed with my friend, Jill in the east dorms. The whole scene with the police and such was just too much for me," she stated.

"I'm just glad it's all over and everyone's ok," Lee Ann said. Connor seemed to give her a skeptical look.

"What? You do think it's over, don't you?" Lee Ann asked.

Connor shrugged. "Did you ever find out about Samantha?"

"Well, Felicity seemed to think that all the manifestations would stop if the bullying stopped. She thinks that Cassie was trying to protect me because she identified with me, having gone through similar experiences herself," Lee Ann shared.

"Hmm, maybe…" Connor expressed. Lee Ann was slightly annoyed at this skepticism. However, as much as she wanted to convince herself that it was over, deep down she too was uncertain.

That night, Lee Ann fell into a deep sleep being physically and emotionally drained from the day before. Her dream started off in the light of late afternoon; she was hiking in the woods, which were vibrant with color and the sounds of birds. She felt reassured as if the place had been lifted from a curse. However, she soon realized that she was back at the spur trail that led to the top of the falls. She saw a young man next to her smiling. A woman suddenly appeared on the trail in front of them. The man tried to get between them but was unable to reach Lee Ann before the young woman put her hands on her and pushed her. The loose rocks gave way beneath Lee Ann's feet, and she realized in horror that she had stumbled backwards and could feel the wet rush of air around her and the rushing noise of the waterfall growing ever closer.

"Noooo!" she yelled, awaking in pool of sweat.

"She didn't jump over the falls, she was pushed!" Lee Ann declared, waking up Connor in the process. "And I might have suffered the same fate if Cassie hadn't intervened."

CHAPTER
FIFTEEN
ABLAZE

The headmaster was uneasy after the day's events. The Haskells had contributed a fortune to the college, and he was worried about their perceptions. The dean's efforts to stop the spread of rumors seemed to him to be woefully inadequate, and he knew that it would be all over campus and beyond by the next day. Unable to sleep, he decided to go to the cabin where the altercation had occurred to investigate for himself. All was quiet as he drove his golf cart through the pathways that led from the administration buildings through the man quad and on to the dorms that bordered the vast forest. He switched off the cart some distance from the dorms so as not to disturb anyone and began to walk down the gravel path towards Gina, Claire, and Becky's cabin. The stillness of the evening was unsettling in and of itself. The wind didn't even stir as a waxing gibbous moon sailed on a still cloud. The night was like a snapshot of a past night being so devoid of activity.

The lights to the cabin were all turned off, but the door had been left unlocked. The headmaster moved slowly and cautiously towards the door as if he expected someone or something to appear at any moment. He turned the knob, pushed the door open and flipped on the light switch, but no lights came on. Something moved outside in the woods about ten yards behind him but there was no rustling in the leaf litter to indicate movement in the forest. Sensing movement, the headmaster turned around and scanned the woods. A shadow passed from tree to tree and vanished.

"Who is there?" the headmaster commanded, unable to contain a slight quiver in his voice. The temperature was dropping, but the man swore it had dropped precipitously in just the last few minutes. He wrapped his arms around himself as he listened for an answer, but none came. He tried to reassure himself by reminding himself that they were on the edge of a very large area of forest with a healthy deer population and even a bear or two. He turned his attention back towards the cabin and cautiously took a few steps inside, leaving the door slightly open should he need to beat a hasty retreat. Everything was just as the girls left it with random articles of clothing, a silver bracelet, a makeup case, and towels strewn about, indicating that they had left in a hurry.

The farthest window closed suddenly, alarming the headmaster. He ran over to it to investigate. There was no one there, but he felt an undeniable chill, much colder than what he had experienced when he was outside a few moments ago. The door slammed shut diverting the headmaster's attention towards the entrance.

"Who is there?" he shouted. He could make out a shadowy figure beginning to form in front of the door and a bright orange light just to its right. The shadow became a fully formed silhouette of a girl with fiery red eyes. In her hand was an object that was on fire as if it had just been set ablaze.

"NO!" the headmaster said, falling to his knees. As the girl moved closer, it became apparent that the flaming object was a book.

"It isn't over!" Cassie cackled. Her features became more apparent as she drew closer. She threw the flaming book onto the large, circular rug in the center of the room, just feet from where the headmaster was crouched down. The rug began to quickly catch fire. The headmaster set his sights on a window to his left. He summoned the courage to get to his feet and open the window. He managed to crawl head-first through the window just in time as the flames spread through the cabin. He ran in a blind panic towards the golf cart, scrambling to call the police as he went. His hands trembled, making it almost impossible to dial the numbers. The flames soon engulfed the entire cabin giving off a tremendous amount of heat that contrasted with the cold night. One by one, the girls in the nearby dorms were awakened as the sirens howled for the second night in a row. Lee Ann and Connor stood on the front patio and watched the fire department put out the flames.

"It's not over," Connor declared. Lee Ann nodded and sighed, feeling both trepidation and disappointment at this turn of events.

"We have got to get her to stop this!" Lee Ann declared as she set off towards the Whispering Falls trailhead.

"Wait for me!" Connor called out behind her.

When Lee Ann reached the overlook, the moon was unveiled from behind the clouds lighting up the proceedings.

"Cassie, I know you're here! Please come and talk with us. We want to help you!" Lee Ann implored.

Lee Ann and Connor stood listening for any response as the sound of the nearby waterfall gushed over the rocks in an endless loop. Finally, they heard a faint voice crying mournfully,

"Andrew? Andrew, where are you?" the voice grew louder. Lee Ann now recognized the slightly raspy sound of Cassie's voice.

"Who is Andrew? Cassie, please tell us. We want to help you!" Lee Ann called out. However, no further response was heard other than the reverberation of the tumbling waters below them.

"Cassie?" Lee Ann called out one last time, but it was clear that Cassie was gone.

Lee Ann knew she had to dig deeper and find out who Samantha and Andrew were. When they got back to the cabin, she began to look back over the newspaper article that she'd found about Cassie and Katy, scanning for anything that she'd missed. Thankfully, she found a quote by one Andrew Johnston whom the article described as Cassie's boyfriend.

"I just can't believe that she would do this. I'm devastated without her," he was quoted as saying in response to the news of her suicide.

"A-ha, I found our Andrew," Lee Ann declared as Connor looked down from her bunk.

"He was her boyfriend." Lee Ann began a more extensive search for him, estimating that his age would now be somewhere around sixty. Sure enough, she soon found a restaurant owner by the name of Andrew Johnston, a graduate from Farthington who lived in the town of Smythe, just thirty minutes away.

"He owns a restaurant called the Iron Bell over in Smythe."

"Ahh!" Connor responded.

"I will be making a trip up there soon to ask him some questions. Tomorrow, I want to go and look in the library for old yearbooks. That would be a great way for us to figure out Samantha's full name. I know now that Cassie was murdered, and we must figure out who is responsible. That is the only way she will ever be at rest."

Connor nodded her head and smiled. She seemed quite pleased at this realization.

Lee Ann could hardly wait to get to the library the next day. It was located halfway across the campus on the west side near the Humanities Department. The library was built in a circular tower with a large bell located on top making it look more medieval than the surrounding buildings although it too was fashioned from pink Georgian marble.

Lee Ann was the only person there aside from the woman behind the desk who was hurriedly checking books back in with a digital scanner.

"We close in an hour due to the early closure of school. Is there something I can help you locate?" she asked. She was a short, stocky middle-aged woman with shoulder length, black hair, and thick-rimmed glasses.

"I really wanted to see some of the old yearbooks or if there is a way for me to access old rosters of students, that would be helpful as well," Lee Ann requested. The woman seemed puzzled by this as if this rarely something that anyone requested.

"This way," she said, leading Lee Ann up the marble staircase to the second floor. There, she turned right into a room full of archives. There were framed photos lining the walls from football games and homecoming dances and the like from a variety of decades.

"The yearbooks are over here. If you want access to student rosters, you will probably have to request that from our records department in the admin building," the woman indicated.

"Thank you," Lee Ann said as her eyes scanned the books. Finally, she found one from 1977-78. Thumbing through the individual photos, she finally managed to find Samantha and lucky for her, there was only one Samantha there that year. Considering it was a small college with a small student body in the late seventies, this was no surprise. Her full name was listed as Samantha Phillips. She had straight blonde hair parted in the middle with flybacks and large, blue eyes.

"Got you!" Lee Ann declared to no one in particular. It was chilling when she stumbled upon the picture of Cassie Rutherford. Cassie had dark, brown eyes, a Betty Paige-style haircut with dyed black hair and dark eye makeup. She seemed to be the only student who decided not to smile for her portrait. Lee Ann found Andrew who was stocky and had dark eyes and light brown hair. Lee Ann felt a sense of familiarity at the sight of these photos, making her think back to the last dream she had at the edge of the waterfall.

That was Andrew and Samantha in the dream. Andrew was there beside me, and Samantha was the one pushing me.

The reality of the events began to sink as Lee Ann realized she was having dreams about things that Cassie experienced directly, reliving them as if they were her own memories. The thought sent a sudden chill through Lee Ann's bones, making her wish she could return to simpler times when she and David would go hiking at one of their favorite spots and didn't have a care in the world. Those times seemed hopelessly out of reach as she found herself in the middle of another unwelcome situation that called for her assistance. She could feel a deep-seated anger growing inside her. She was angry about what had happened to Cassie, for what she was having to endure instead of a normal freshman year of college, and at her father for forcing her to go Farthington.

I never would have even been put in this situation if it weren't for Dad, she thought to herself as she made her way back to the cabin. As Lee Ann was walking back, Julie came driving up in her golf cart, waving to her.

"Hey, how are you?" Julie asked.

"Been better, but thanks for asking!" Lee Ann said.

"I've got some news. First off, the Dean has called the girls into the office about the cafeteria incident. I'm not sure what the outcome of the meeting was yet, but I'll let you know if I hear of anything. Also, beginning tomorrow, the college is going to close early for the winter break because of the disturbances that have been taking place," Julie shared. It was odd not to see her smiling as she usually was.

"Wow," Lee Ann responded simply.

"What do you think is going on? There are all kinds of rumors floating around about you and the old story about Cassie. I've told everyone I can that it is not like you to harass someone. I told them that there must be another explanation. Some people believe that it's not you at all, but the spirit of Cassie seeking revenge or trying to get Gina to stop bullying you."

"Well, I don't want to alarm you, but I have it on good authority that the latter is true, although I'm still trying to figure out what happened to Cassie and how we can help her to move on."

"Wow, well I guess you would know," Julie remarked.

"Yeah, guess so," Lee Ann said.

"Well, I'm off to pack. Got a three-hour plane ride ahead later today. Try and have a great winter break!" Julie said.

"You too, and thanks so much for standing up for me, Julie. You're the best!" Lee Ann stated.

"Don't mention it! See you soon!" Julie answered with a wave as she drove off in her gold cart.

ALTHOUGH THE WINTER break was still a couple of weeks away, the college decided that it was too risky to remain open after what had just taken place. Despite the best efforts of the PR department, the story of the mysterious goings on at Farthington had leaked to the outside world. Some of the news outlets reported the possible supernatural connection with the events while others painted the picture of a stalker and arsonist who was terrorizing the dorms. Either way, it was a complete public relations disaster for Farthington College. The phones were ringing off the hook with parents demanding an explanation for what had been happening, wondering why security had not been sufficient to prevent such occurrences. Some were threatening not to pay tuition that semester or worse, still declared that their son or daughter would be withdrawing after the semester concluded. Headmaster Blevins began to call the parents one by one explaining how they were doing everything they could to ensure the ongoing safety of the students and catch whoever was responsible for the disturbances

CHAPTER

SIXTEEN

RESPITE

Charles pulled up into the parking lot at Farthington. Lee Ann opened the back door of the familiar, now somewhat rusted, red pickup truck and threw her bags into the back seat. She jumped into the front passenger seat and looked over at her father's grave expression as he pulled out of the parking space.

"I owe you an apology," he said in a tone that matched his expression.

"For what?" Lee Ann was puzzled even though she had to admit she liked where this was going.

"I never should have forced you to go to Farthington. Now I get this call from the headmaster about possible arson on the campus and that you're getting bullied by a bunch of snobby girls."

"None of that is your fault," Lee Ann conceded.

"I know, Lee Ann, but none of this would have happened if I'd listened to you in the first place and respected your wishes. I just wanted to do what I thought was best and what I thought was best for your future. I shouldn't have been so concerned with your grades considering what's been goin' on," Charles explained.

"Look, I'll admit that I was pretty pissed at you for a minute, but I understand that you were only doing what you thought was right for me. I get it, being an artist can be a tenuous thing without guaranteed income and the odds of finding success aren't great. If I had a kid and they told me they wanted to be an artist, I'm unsure as to how I would even react."

"Well, you put it that way, I might need to change my mind," Charles joked. Lee Ann laughed and gave him a light punch on his right arm as they passed through bucolic scenes of forested hillsides and fields.

"Just how bad is it gettin', punkin?"

"Pretty bad. Cassie is wreaking havoc. I thought she might be appeased when the bullying stopped, but that's before I realized that she had been pushed off the cliff. She didn't jump."

"How do you know for sure?"

"Well, I told you about the dreams I've been having. I had another one recently where I was pushed off the cliff. I think it's Cassie trying to show me what happened to her," Lee Ann shared.

"Wouldn't it be nice if she just told you?" Charles remarked.

"Ha! I wish. Everything seems cryptic with the spirit world for whatever reason," Lee Ann said, shaking her head.

Her heart felt lifted as she began to see familiar landscapes near their land. She could feel the anger towards her father melting away replaced with affection and understanding for him. She smiled at him and took his cap and put it on herself.

"You sure seem like you're doing pretty good, considering!" Charles commented.

"I am, now that we're going home," she said with a laugh.

David was standing there on the front porch with his hands in his pockets as they reached the end of the drive. Shirley was just inside, preparing a homecoming lunch. Lee Ann thought about how David looked like he had put on a pound or two, but he was the same boy she had loved for so long with the same bad posture and bangs that hung into his dark eyes.

As soon as they got out of the truck, David ran over and opened the door for Lee Ann. The two of them stared at one another taking each other in to make up for lost time; they kissed and embraced for several minutes. Charles blushed and went into the house to help Shirley.

"They really missed each other. Remember when we would get that way?" Shirley reminisced as she observed the happy couple through the window.

"You mean we're not that way anymore?" Charles asked, jokingly. He came up behind her, wrapped his arms around her and kissed the back of the neck.

"Ok, I guess we're still that way. Lucky us," Shirley answered.

"I apologized to her, Shirl," Charles admitted.

"For what?" she asked.

"For making her go to Farthington and not listening to her," he answered. Shirley turned to look him in the eye.

"Charles Daniels, I am so proud of you!" she announced, making him laugh.

"I'm serious honey. You've come a long way. There was a time when I couldn't get you to apologize for anything."

"Was I really that bad?" he asked, making a pouty face. Shirley laughed and nodded. They both continued to laugh together.

David and Lee Ann walked hand in hand on a trail that led around the back of the property behind the house.

"I want you to come home," David suddenly said after staring off into space for a moment.

"I can't come home yet, David," Lee Ann answered.

"Why not? The situation is getting dangerous for you," he urgently stated, turning to face her.

"It was dangerous the last time too, at Thief's Hollow," she reminded him.

"Yes, but it's different this time. Like Felicity said, this girl or spirit girl has attached to you for some reason. She's volatile, Lee Ann," he pointed out.

"Yes, and that's why I have to try and help her. If I don't try and put a stop to this, then who else will?"

"Why is it your duty to clean up their ghost problem?" David implored.

"David, I've been trying to run from this gift I possess that attracts these spirits to me. But the more I try and run, the more it comes back to nag me," she explained.

"Cassie was pushed off that cliff and I must find out exactly what happened and why it was made to look like a suicide. I think that's why she hasn't found peace. She can't move on because she's holding on to what happened to her. Justice was not served. Everyone at Farthington just wants to sweep the whole thing under the rug and act like nothing ever happened. As much as I dislike Gina, I would not want to see her or anyone else get hurt or worse."

David stared at her for a long time. He knew her well enough to know her determination. At that moment, he realized that he was not going to be able to convince her to alter her course of action.

"Ok but let me help you. I want to come back to Farthington with you. I can stay in a nearby town if I have to. We should all go and help just like last time. You need us," he pointed out.

"I need to do a bit of detective work. I'm going to contact Cassie's former boyfriend who may be able to tell me a lot about what happened the night of Cassie's death, if he's willing to talk to me."

Felicity came by later that evening for dinner. After they finished eating, Felicity went out on the back patio with Lee Ann so that the two of them could talk alone.

"So, how are you?" Felicity asked her.

"I'm hanging in there, but Cassie is really getting out of control," Lee Ann pointed out.

"Yes, I can see I was wrong to think that she would be appeased if Gina stopped bullying you. She is restless because her death was unjust. What she needs is for the truth to be revealed about what happened to her and for those that are responsible to be held accountable," Felicity stated.

"Will you come and help me again? I don't think I can do this on my own," Lee Ann pleaded.

"Yes, I will be there. What about Jasmine and Katrina? The more support you gather, the better."

"They're coming over in a bit; hopefully they can come as well."

"I'm just glad that no one has been harmed, but this continues to be a very dangerous situation. Cassie's anger is growing in power, but one thing that will help is you and the change I sense in you," Felicity observed.

"What do you mean?"

"You have released so much of your anger that you are harboring although I sense that you are still holding onto some."

"I'm angry at the situation now. I'm angry that I can't just go back to school and finish out the semester like a normal student, focusing on my classes and my grade point average, not some drama from forty something years ago," Lee Ann opined.

"But you're not angry with Charles anymore?"

"No, not really. I realize now that he was only doing what he thought was best. He feels terrible about what's happened and feels responsible for putting me in harm's way. It's sweet. I can't stay mad at him," Lee Ann admitted.

"Well, that's great and I think it may help the situation. You see, I have a theory that your presence, your anger coupled with your situation with Gina has caused a flare up so to speak. That energy has attracted Cassie. Her anger is fed by your own because of the connection she has made with you."

"And how do I undo this connection?"

"Well, letting go of the anger is an important first step because the anger clouds your judgment and keeps you from being in your truth and being your full self, and as I stated before, it fuels her anger. In order for us to help Cassie move on, we have to first figure out what exactly happened to her and who kept the truth from coming out. If we bring everything into the light, then we may be able to help Cassie move on." Felicity smiled, comforting Lee Ann with her confidence and calm demeanor. Lee Ann was always amazed at Felicity's ability to maintain a clear head and inner peace. Lee Ann pictured Felicity sitting calmly, unscathed and smiling in the middle of a hurricane while debris and chaos ensued all around her.

"Believe it or not, I once felt the same as you as a young woman. I didn't want the gifts I'd be given, although in all fairness it wasn't as intense as what you've experienced although I certainly could feel energetic presences. I wanted to live a normal life like everyone else and went to school far from home, thinking that would make a difference. It didn't. When I tried to silence the voices, I had to insist that they give me the space that I need and set up a specific place and time for me to hear their concerns. Once I embraced my gifts and set up some boundaries, I was much happier. Rejecting your gifts will not stop those in need from reaching out to you. There is no way to prevent them from seeking you out like a moth to a bright light."

"Why is death so messy? I mean, it seems like the transition from this world to the next is very chaotic. Many people don't know they've passed on, and if they do figure that out, half the time they don't seem to know what to do."

"It is messy, but that is why we have been chosen. We are spiritual guides of a sort if you will as I think you understand by now even if you don't understand the whys."

Lee Ann felt her strength and confidence returning. She felt as if a weight has been lifted with respect to her situation as she saw Jasmine and Katrina pull up in Katrina's green Volkswagen bug.

The two friends ran up and hugged Lee Ann.

"I've missed you guys so much!" Lee Ann declared.

"We're here now! Sorry to hear that Cassie's on a tear," Katrina announced.

"Yeah, you just can't seem to catch a break," Jasmine added.

"Well, seeing you guys again lets me know that I do possess the strength to face this thing with your help of course."

"We got your back," David said as he slid his arm around Lee Ann and kissed her check.

CHAPTER
SEVENTEEN
LOOSE THREADS

The desolation of winter had set in at Farthington when Charles drove Lee Ann back to campus. The hills were now covered with leafless, gnarled branches reaching for the sky. The clouds rolled over the sky in a thick blanket that promised no sunshine. The still, grey landscape matched Lee Ann's dread.

"You don't have to do this you know?" Charles said as they stepped out of the truck and looked out over the campus.

"I know, but we've been through this. If we don't do something, Cassie may really hurt someone," Lee Ann replied.

It was still a week before classes were set to resume, but students had been given the go ahead to return after a thorough investigation had been conducted. There was no evidence of arson other than the building itself. The headmaster had also just moved back onto campus and had hired his own personal security guard for his living quarters, just south of the administration buildings near the wood's edge.

Katrina and Jasmine pulled up at the same time, while David followed just behind them in his pickup. Felicity arrived a few minutes later. The plan was for Lee Ann's friends to stay in the nearby town of Smythe, which is where the nearest motel was located. The families were allowed to come on campus for the next week to help students move in and such.

"Hoping that you guys will finally get to meet my roommate, Connor," Lee Ann said as everyone followed her down the leaf-strewn path that led to the cabins. Lee Ann was surprised to see that there was no trace of her roommate even though Connor told her that she expected to be back by that time.

"Huh, well, I guess you guys may never meet her," Lee Ann shrugged and went to turn on the heat. Felicity looked around, worriedly.

"Are you ok?" Lee Ann asked.

"Yes, it's just that, well that presence that I felt the last time has not abated," she reported.

"I'm sure that's the case, but with all of you here, I feel so much better like the clouds have lifted!" Lee Ann announced.

"That's great! Try and hold that if you can because it will not be easy to assuage the level of betrayal and hostility I feel with this presence. Why don't we chase down some loose threads? I think it's time we talk to this boyfriend of Cassie's.

"Well, we shouldn't all go. That would probably be pretty intimidating," Lee Ann pointed out.

"Right, let's you and I go," Felicity suggested.

"I want to go with you!" David insisted. Lee Ann walked over to him and kissed him lightly on the cheek.

"Felicity's right. We'll be back as soon as we can," Lee Ann assured him.

"Hey, tell you what. I will pay for everyone else to go to another restaurant in town. I'm starved!" Charles declared.

"There is no other restaurant in that town," Lee Ann informed him.

Katrina got out her smart phone to scan for restaurants near them.

"Hmm, let's see. How about The Lantern over in Coburn? It says they have the best home cooking in the state of Tennessee. If it says it, then it must be true. It's only fifteen minutes away," she reported.

"Sounds good! Well, see you back here a little later," Charles declared, thinking with his stomach. "Oh, and be careful!"

"Will do, dad!" Lee Ann answered. She went over to David and kissed him again.

"See you later, ok?" she whispered.

"Ok, do be careful," David whispered back.

The dreary conditions continued as Felicity and Lee Ann made the ten-minute drive north to Smythe.

"Do you think it would do any good to try and get Cassie to tell us more about what would appease her?" Lee Ann inquired.

"Well, it wouldn't hurt, but don't' expect direct answers. She may not know herself. You see, often the disembodied don't even know what it is that they're holding onto that's keeping them from transitioning. That's part of what our task is, to realize what it is and then help Cassie to see it. I have a feeling that your presence at Farthington awakened her and that she isn't at rest because of the unjust circumstances surrounding her death. If those responsible are held accountable, she may be assuaged."

"Let's hope so. My grade point average can't take another semester like the first one," Lee Ann pointed out.

"Don't be so hard on yourself. You are doing the best you can under very challenging circumstances. Try and remember that." Felicity's words washed over Lee Ann and comforted her.

They reached the restaurant which was busy with the late lunch crowd. The building resembled a rustic store front, like something out of a wild west set. There was a rusty iron bell just above the painted sign with the same name in wild west font.

A horseshoe hung just above the large, wooden door.

"Well, that's a good sign, I guess," Lee Ann joked as they walked in.

There was a large buffet set up in the main room with tables and booths scattered throughout the main room and several smaller rooms. It looked like it had once been a grand hotel that had been converted. Felicity and Lee Ann sat down at a smaller farm table in the corner of the room, near the buffet. A waitress came up to them almost as soon as they sat down.

"What can I get y'all to drink?" she asked in a thick drawl. She took a pen from behind her ear and placed a small pad on the table.

"Just water please," Felicity requested.

"Sweet tea, and also we would like to speak to the manager if he's here," Lee Ann asked, cutting to the chase.

"Is everything alright?" the waitress asked, sounding concerned.

"Oh yes, we just wanted to complement him on such a well-run establishment," Felicity answered to put the woman's mind at ease.

"I'll go see if he's available, and I'll be back with your drinks in a sec," she answered, hurrying away towards the back.

For a long time, no one came, so Lee Ann and Felicity decided to try the buffet. Normally, Lee Ann wasn't much of a fan of buffets as she used to say that there was no way to know for sure how long some of the food had been sitting under the heat lamps. However, the food was being brought out very often due to how fast people were gobbling it up. It was obviously a favorite Sunday afternoon restaurant. Almost everyone other than Lee Ann and Felicity was dressed in their Sunday best.

After about fifteen minutes, a man around sixty-five came over to the table. He was balding and well dressed, but unable to hide a prominent gut.

"Are you young ladies having a fine experience today? Carla said you wanted to talk with me?" The man had a very formal, slow southern accent that reminded Lee Ann of the deep south.

"Yes, first off let me say how delicious these vegetables are. This is the best squash casserole I've ever had!" Felicity said, thinking it best to start with a polite complement.

"Well, thanks! All our vegetables are grown right here in Bryant County. Nothing frozen here," he said with a smile.

"My name's Andrew and let me know if there's anything I can do for you," he said, preparing to walk away.

"Well, there is one more thing," Lee Ann shared.

"Yes, young lady?" Andrew asked.

"Did you know a girl named Cassie Rutherford?" Lee Ann blurted out.

The man looked as if someone had just handed him some really bad news.

"Cassie? Who are you?" he said, sounding irritated.

"I'm a student at Farthington," Lee Ann informed him. "Cassie isn't at rest. She's wreaking havoc on the campus, and we think someone might get hurt. Please help us. We are just trying to understand what happened to her so that we can help her and everyone at Farthington find peace," Lee Ann pleaded.

"She committed suicide! What do you mean she's not at rest? I'm not sure what you're suggesting, but you aren't welcome here. Get out of my restaurant!" he insisted in such a loud tone, all the nearby tables could hear him.

"I mean it! Get out and don't come back to the Iron Bell, ever!" Andrew yelled before hurrying back to the office in the back.

"We had better leave," Felicity said.

"I know, but hold on a sec," Lee Ann said. She took the pen that the waitress had left and write a note on the napkin.

Please have Andrew contact me if he wishes to help us. We urgently need any information he might have that could help us bring Cassie peace. My name is Lee Ann Daniels and my number is 615- 768-0923

"It was worth a shot," Lee Ann stated as they hurriedly left the restaurant while all eyes were trained on them. Many of the families were whispering amongst themselves about what just took place.

"Wow, that was so suspicious," Lee Ann remarked on the ride back to Farthington.

"Yes, he is obviously harboring some deep-seated guilt. We may have to figure out what happened without his assistance," Felicity bemoaned.

"I want to find this Samantha next," Lee Ann suggested.

"Yes, however getting her to talk to us will likely be even harder than getting Andrew to," Felicity lamented.

"We must try even if it's all for naught. We have to do what we can for Cassie," Lee Ann stated.

Felicity smiled at her. "You know something, you have really come a long way since I've known you, Lee Ann Daniels. You have become such a thoughtful, considerate young woman, much more even tempered and less self-centered than the teenager I met two and a half years ago," Felicity shared.

"Thanks, I guess," Lee Ann laughed.

CHAPTER
EIGHTEEN
VISITATIONS

Headmaster Blevins paced back and forth like a caged animal, stopping by one of the windows every few minutes to look out as if he expected Cassie to be there. A security guard was on constant watch outside of his living quarters ever since the cabin burned down and could clearly be seen walking the perimeter. It was two-thirty in the morning, and he'd been pacing like that for two hours contemplating his current situation. There were at least twenty threats that parents had made over the last couple of weeks to withdraw their students from Farthington if the school didn't get to the bottom of the situation. Most troubling was Gina's father's threats to withdraw their generous contribution to the school. Headmaster Blevins had sent out an email detailing how the police had come up with no evidence of arson, and that it was safe for everyone to return to campus, although he knew that this wasn't in fact the case with Cassie still roaming around. Now there was nothing to do but wait and see who would make good on their threats and try to reassure everyone.

Finally, he grew too weary to pace any longer and sat down on the edge of the bed, feeling his eyelids growing ever heavier. After a few moments of nodding off, he focused on an object that he hadn't noticed only moments before, sitting on the coffee table nearby. It was a book, one that was familiar to him. It had a flowery cover and was greatly worn as if to suggest it was very old and had been often used by its former owner like a journal or diary. Suddenly, a burst of wind shot through the window, opened the book and ruffled its pages.

"NO!" the headmaster said, getting to his feet.

"I already destroyed you!" he declared.

He grabbed the book off the table and headed into the sitting room where a fire was ablaze in the hearth. He threw the book into the fire and carefully watched the pages blacken and smolder, making sure that it was well and truly destroyed. Just to be sure, he scraped up what was left of the ashes and placed them into a paper bag. He took it outside, looking around him to see if anyone was about, including the security guard who was nowhere to be found. He stopped by a storage shed in the back and took out a rusty shovel. He took the bag and the shovel and walked a few yards into the dark wood behind his living quarters. Only a few crickets and the rustle of the wind was there to greet him. He dug a hole as deep as he could and threw the bag into it, covering up as quickly and carefully as he could, making sure to spread leaves over the spot. He paused for a moment and looked back towards the light of his home having heard some movement. He half expected the security guard to emerge, but no one did. The headmaster turned back towards the spot where he had buried the book and was astonished to see the book sitting there on the spot unscathed. Its flowery cover stared at him mockingly, defying physics and logic.

"No, NO! How can this be?" he shouted. In a fit of rage and desperation, he began to tear pages from the book and throw them all around him into the leaf litter of the forest floor. He heard a sound coming from the direction of the house again, closer this time and turned to face the noise.

" Who's there? What do you want?" Despite his shaky hands and growing fear, he emerged from the wood and began to walk towards the house. A shadow passed between the headmaster and his home. He ran in that direction.

"Show yourself!" he commanded, but no one answered. The sound of crunching leaves could then be heard behind him in the woods. He ran back in that direction to face whomever it was, but found himself alone, enveloped by the darkness.

"Why do you torment me?" he demanded, unable to hide the fear in his voice.

"I know what you did!" a female voice hissed just behind him. The headmaster fell backwards onto the forest floor and turned to face the voice from where he had fallen. There was the transparent, wretched form of Cassie, looking down on him with an explosive rage.

"I know what you did!" she hissed again, drawing closer.

"I did it, yes, I did it. I burned the book, so that no one would see what Samantha wrote! I'm so sorry! Please forgive me!'

This prompted a wicked, high-pitched laugh from Cassie that grew to such a piercing volume in the headmaster's ears, he had to put his fingers in them.

"NO!!!!!!" he yelled to drown out the laughter, causing himself to sit up in his bed in the process and realize that he'd just awoken from one hell of a nightmare. He was covered in sweat, but to his relief, there was no sound except a gentle breeze blowing outside a slightly open window. Headmaster Blevins went to the window and looked out. He was pleased to see the security guard standing on the front porch looking at the night sky.

ANDREW TOOK a deep breath as he waited just outside of the back door of the Iron Bell restaurant. Only Jennifer, a waitress was still inside. He was waiting for her to get her things so that he could lock up for the evening. Although he hadn't smoked a cigarette in over two years, he began to have a craving begin to gnaw at him that he couldn't deny.

"Sorry it took me so long, I couldn't remember where I left my phone," Jennifer spoke as she came through the door. She was medium height with her dark brown hair tied up in a ponytail.

"Oh, it's ok. Look, I know I quit and all, but do you happen to have one of those camels you're always smoking?" he asked. The look in his eyes worried Jennifer. In the five years that she'd been working there, she'd never seen him look so pale and distant.

"You ok, boss?" she asked him.

"Eh, yeah," he answered like he was snapping back from a trance. "Long day."

"Yeah, here ya go," she said, reluctantly handing him a smoke. She lit it for him and looked him up and down.

"It's those women that came in today," she blurted out.

Andrew's eyes grew wide as he sat down in a fold out chair that had been placed there for workers on their smoke break.

"Yes. They reminded me of something that happened a long, long time ago. An old girlfriend of mine that died," he related. He had meant to keep this to himself, but it all came flowing out of him when Jennifer mentioned it.

"Oh my, I'm so sorry," she said, coming over to pat him on the back.

"Thanks," he said as tears began to flow from his eyes uncontrollably. Jennifer was shocked. She'd never seen him like this. He was usually very stoic and level-headed. In fact, there had been many occasions when she was having personal issues and he'd been the one to offer advice and word of comfort.

"It's ok," she said, handing him a tissue from her purse.

"I'm so sorry, I better get going," he said, getting up from the chair as he wiped his eyes.

"Yeah, me too. Are you going to be ok?" she asked.

"Yeah, I just need a good night's sleep. Thanks for listening, Jenn. Oh, and please not a word..."

"Don't worry, boss. This is between us. I just want you to know that I'm sorry for your loss even if it was a long time ago," she offered.

"Thanks, that means a lot," he answered.

He walked the two blocks between the restaurant and his home trying to think of anything but Cassie, but he couldn't. His mind kept going back to earlier that day when Felicity and Lee Ann confronted him.

Why is this happening now after all these years? It can't be her, can it? But how else would those two women know about her?

Not even half a bottle of Jack Daniels could free his mind from the events of forty- four years ago. He finally dozed off in his favorite lounge chair with the television still on. He came to an hour later, awoken by his own snores. On his way to the bathroom, he sensed some movement behind him. He turned around but couldn't find any evidence of anything, so he shrugged it off and went to the bathroom. While , something moved past the open doorway; this time it was undeniable.

"Who's here?" he slurred, but no one answered. Andrew's first thought was to get to the Glock pistol that he kept in his bedside drawer. He ran down the hall to the bedroom, but something or someone slammed the door in his face before he could get inside. Laughter issued from the air above him.

"What do you want?" he yelled, cowering on the floor.

A shadow suddenly appeared and began to materialize into Cassie's angry visage. She was so close; Andrew could make out the now torn fishnets and ripped black leather skirt and a dingy Clash t-shirt that she wore on that day so long ago, but what shook him the most was the glowing, red-hot malice in her dark eyes that were surrounded by black eyeliner that had run down both sides of her transparent face.

"You should know by now!" she hissed in an otherworldly voice soaked with reverberation.

"Ok, ok. I can't carry this with me any longer. I'm so, so sorry Cassie!"

"Too late for all that, Andrew!" She smiled at him, but this was somehow more unsettling because it was a smile of wicked satisfaction. She was gone as soon as she appeared as Andrew opened his eyes and realized he was still in his chair in the living room. He pinched himself to make sure, but he knew he was finally conscious, and now he knew what he had to do.

The next day, Lee Ann's friends all met up with her at the cabin to discuss their next move.

"No matter how hard I search, I cannot find any record of a Samantha Ryan," Lee Ann reported to the others. Katrina and Jasmine were playing chess. David was sitting beside her, and Felicity was meditating on a blanket in the corner.

"Maybe she got married," Jasmine suggested.

"Ah, but to ? What we need is the town purveyor of gossip" Katrina asked no one in particular.

"How do we find that out?" David bemoaned.

Felicity opened her eyes and took a deep breath before speaking.

"I would bet that our friend, Andrew knows," she finally said.

"Too bad he won't give us the time of day," Lee Ann moaned. Just then a text came in on Lee Ann's phone that lay on the desk beside her laptop. She picked it up and read the message aloud.

Hi, this is Andrew Johnston. I apologize for being rude before but I'm ready to talk to you. Meet me at the restaurant at 9:30 PM tomorrow if you can make it.

"I can't believe it! I wonder what changed his mind?" Lee Ann wondered.

"He likely has a lot to unburden himself of; secrets he has harbored for years and years that have eaten away at him," Felicity mused.

"Or Cassie somehow got to him," Katrina joked, but no one laughed because they all secretly wondered if she indeed had gotten to him.

CHAPTER
NINETEEN
RECOLLECTION

Felicity and Lee Ann pulled up in the parking lot of the Iron Bell Restaurant as the last of the staff was pulling out of the parking lot. Andrew came out of the front door looking from side to side as if he wanted to make sure no one was still around.

"Come on in," Andrew welcomed them. The look on his face was quite different from the angry expression he wore the first time they met him. Now, he looked forlorn and worried like a huge weight was pulling down on him.

"Thank you so much for agreeing to speak with us," Felicity said as Andrew motioned for them to take a seat at one of the booths.

"Can I get either of you anything?" he asked.

"No, I'm good," Lee Ann answered.

"Nothing for me, thank you," Felicity replied.

"Look, I want to apologize for the way I acted when you two first came here. There was no excuse for it," Andrew began, taking a seat opposite them in the booth.

"Well, it's a lot to take in when complete strangers come into your restaurant and start asking questions about situations that they shouldn't know anything about," Felicity allowed.

"So, let's start there. How do you know about Cassie?" he inquired.

Lee Ann and Felicity proceeded to tell him everything that had been occurring since Lee Ann's arrival.

"My God," Andrew said, his face looking drained of blood.

"After all these years she is still not at rest, and I'm partially to blame for it," he said as tears began to well up in his eyes. His vulnerability and regret gained Felicity and Lee Ann's sympathies.

"Take your time and unburden yourself of the past. You have to let go of the secrets that are eating at you. I can see it," Felicity said, sympathetically.

Andrew took a deep breath and nodded.

"I want to tell you everything so that justice can be served. After all these years, I feel almost hollowed out inside. Secrets will slowly eat away at you like that. I tried my best to stuff it down and forget, but it would always come creeping back, usually in the dead of night when I'm trying to sleep. Anyway, I came to Farthington in '76 as a business major. After a few months, I met Samantha Rogers, who was one of the more popular girls on campus. Her father gave lots of money to the school and it was well known that her family was doing well for themselves. We began to date and did so for about eight months. As I got to know Samantha better, I liked her less and less. She was superficial and petty and used to talk badly about other girls to make herself feel better. All that got worse when Cassie and Katie came to the school in '77."

"What was it about their arrival that made things worse?" Lee Ann asked.

"Well, it was a bit of jealousy mixed with the fear of the unknown. You see, Cassie and Katie were what you'd call punk girls. They wore leather jackets and black t-shirts and dyed their hair. All of that was really new at the time and a lot of people were threatened by it even though both Cassie and Katie were nice as they could be. A lot of the guys thought they were attractive, which didn't sit well with many of the girls. Cassie and Katie immediately became targets for Samantha and her friends, especially Cassie because she put herself out there more. Katie mostly stayed in her dorm and read.

Anyway, the more the bullying went on, the less I wanted to be with Samantha. After repeatedly asking her to stop her behavior, Samantha became enraged thinking that I was sweet on Cassie. To tell the truth, I was beginning to like her after we had a history class together. All of this came to a head one day when Samantha saw me talking to Cassie after class. We fought, and I broke up with Samantha. A couple weeks later, I asked Cassie out and we began to see each other."

Lee Ann was struck by the parallels between Andrew's story and her experiences with Gina and her friends.

Andrew paused to take a sip of water and continued, "So, after I began to see Cassie, the bullying only intensified. Samantha would stop at nothing, taking every opportunity she could to try and humiliate and embarrass Cassie. Despite all of that, Cassie and I were happy together and spent as much time away from the others as we could. One of our favorite things to do was hike up to the top of Whispering Falls." The mention of this made Andrew choke up, and his story was interrupted by low, muffled sobs. He apologized as he wiped his eyes with a napkin and took a deep breath.

"I really loved her," he confessed.

"It's ok, take your time," Felicity said, patting his hand gently.

"So, one day we hiked up to the top of the falls like we often did to watch the sunset. Little did we know that Samantha and her friend had also decided to take the same hike that day. While we were standing there watching the sunset, we heard the voices of people coming from down the trail. We turned to see Samantha and one of her friends, Patricia, I believe it was, coming towards us. It was very heated. Samantha began to go off on the two of us while I yelled for her to stop. She began shouting at Cassie about how she had stolen her man and lunged at her suddenly. We were standing very close to the overlook. I tried to get in between them, but it all happened so fast..." he began to trail off into sobs again, unable to contain himself.

"So, it's true then, she didn't commit suicide," Lee Ann clarified.

"No, she was pushed off the edge by Samantha," he confirmed.

It took several moments before Andrew was composed enough to continue with the story.

"I really don't think that Samantha really meant to kill Cassie. I think she pushed her out of anger at a moment when she wasn't thinking clearly and had lost control. I mean, Samantha was a lot of things, but not a murderer," Andrew said, shaking his head.

"What happened next?" Lee Ann inquired.

"Samantha was hysterical. She couldn't believe what she'd done and what had happened. She begged me and Patricia repeatedly not to tell anyone what had happened. I screamed at her and ran down the trail as fast as I could with her running after me. When I got back to campus, I immediately began to make my way towards the campus security office to tell them everything that had happened. Samantha caught up to me before I could get there. Headmaster Blevins saw the two of us just outside the administration building. He asked us what we were so upset about and told us to come back to his office.

When we got there, I told him everything that had happened and that I was going to the police. He warned me that if I took drastic actions like that, I could kiss my fully paid scholarship goodbye. He even threatened to accuse me of pushing Cassie and that it would be my word against theirs. In the end, I couldn't find a way out of the situation, so Samantha and I agreed that we would never tell anyone what had happened and get Patricia to agree to this as well, which she did. So, the headmaster painted a picture of a troubled, suicidal punk girl. It didn't help matters when Katie jumped over the falls a week later. She was unable to cope with the grief of losing her best friend. Then the story transformed into a sordid tale of a suicidal punk cult that of course, didn't exist."

Felicity and Lee Ann did not speak for several minutes, trying to digest the tragic tale that he had shared with them.

"Are you willing to share your story with the authorities?" Lee Ann finally asked.

"Yes, there is nothing that I would like more than to get this off my chest. I don't believe I've had a good night's sleep for forty years. I don't even care what happens to me at this point. Anything is better than having to live with this one more day." The darkened circles around Andrew's eyes were evidence of his tortured nights. "Thing is, I'm not sure that they will believe us or do much about it after all these years. That case was closed right after everything happened. Everyone just accepted the headmaster's explanation and went on with their lives. It was easy for people around here to believe that a punk girl would do something like that or even be a part of a cult. Hell, everyone practically thought punk was a cult thing when it first started."

"What we need is a confession from Samantha," Felicity stated.

"Yes, but how in the world would we ever get her to agree to such a thing?" Lee Ann complained.

"If Samantha's dreams are anything like the ones I've been having recently, I bet she might come around," Andrew confessed. He went on to tell them about his recent dream in which Cassie paid him a visit.

"I have a feeling that she will, too," Felicity shared. "Never underestimate the unrequited yearning of a life cut too short. We can only hope that we can assuage her by exposing the truth."

CHAPTER
TWENTY
REGRET

S amantha Hampton paced back and forth on her back deck looking out at the view of the surrounding hillsides. Normally this view brought her peace of mind at the end of a long day, but today it brought back the distant memory of regrets that still sat heavy in her subconscious. Her husband, Harold was already asleep, and even the sound of his snoring which usually annoyed her, couldn't pervade the mood she was in. It had been months since she had thought about the events at Farthington, but something was bringing everything back to her.

It was an accident. I never really intended to push her. She reassured herself the same way she had for years when the memory would return, trying to justify her actions. It would stave off her guilt for the moment but would return at the strangest times like a nagging toothache that comes and goes intermittently.

Let's try and get some sleep. You have to give that presentation during the board meeting in the morning.

Although it was hard because of Harold's persistent snoring, she managed to finally get to sleep after about an hour of tossing and turning. Not long after she fell asleep, she found herself back on the familiar trail to Whispering Falls, making her way up the steep climb towards the end of the hike. At that moment, she held no memory of the events that had occurred there decades before. The sun shone down, illuminating the various shades of green in the forest and the birds kept up their usual chatter.

When she reached the top, it seemed alarming to her how quickly the light had begun to fade away. The sunset was already ending as its colors bled just above the horizon; above it was cloak of night draping itself over the remains of the dying light.

Why is the light fading so quickly? She had enough wherewithal to realize that the scene unfolding before her was unnatural. The emotion coming over her was not unlike the fear that animals sometimes feel when a storm is imminent, unsettled by the drop in the pressure and a pervading sense of dread. Nonetheless, she kept moving forward towards the edge of the falls that roared to her right. She stopped a few feet from the ledge observing the splashing of the water on the rocks below and uniformity of the white, lacey spray of water that fell slowly through the air.

Samantha was torn from this moment by a hand that reached over from the edge of the cliff and grabbed her ankle with a powerful, painful grip. It pulled with an incredible amount of strength that threw Samantha off balance, causing her to fall on her back. Her hands scrambled for something to hold onto, pulling at plants and rocks as she slid towards the edge. Her ears were filled with Cassie's sinister laughter.

"Time to confess!" Cassie announced. Her words resounded in the grotto like it had been played from a loudspeaker.

"Ok, ok, just make it all stop!" Samantha pleaded. Her legs were now dangling over the edge of the cliff, but she had managed to grab onto a tree root.

"I...I did it. I pushed you over the cliff because I was jealous of you...." Samantha pleaded.

"Not to me, you idiot. It's time to pay for what you've done. You must confess your crimes to everyone and face the consequences... Or else."

Samantha felt icy, unseen fingers loosening her grip on the tree root. She began to slide over the edge again, feeling first her body hurtling into gravity's embrace as the water soaked her body.

"NOOOOO!" She awoke with a start, her husband gripped the covers and stared at her, mouth agape.

"Honey, you ok?" He asked.

"No! No, I'm not, Harold. I can't keep pushing this down and thinking I can live with it."

Harold knew Samantha's secret. She'd confided in him one night after several glasses of wine when they had been married a little over a year. Sharing everything with him made it a little bit easier for Samantha to live with herself. Harold handled the news stoically, but deep down he was unsettled to hear that her wife was capable of such things. Nonetheless he agreed to keep her secret and tried to ignore his own feelings when they nagged at him.

"What happened?"

"It was Cassie. She's back. I can't explain how or anything, but she is not at rest."

"What do you mean?" Harold asked.

"Harold, she tried to pull me over the edge. She wants me to confess..."

"That's just your conscience. It makes an appearance every few years and goes away again..."

"No, no, it's not my conscience, Harold. You have to trust me on this. It was her. Something about the whole experience was unlike any dream I've ever had. It was just too real..."

"Now look, hun. You have a huge presentation to give in the morning. I think maybe your stress over that has recalled some old skeletons from the closet," he said, patting her on the shoulder.

She was torn between being agitated over his mansplaining and wanting to agree to his perspective.

"Maybe you're right..." Samantha conceded. Harold seemed

satisfied by this. He flashed her a quick smile, kissed her briefly and rolled over to go back to sleep.

Despite her efforts, Samantha was unable to get back to sleep; instead she stared at the ceiling the whole night through, trying to clear her nagging conscience.

BACK AT THE CABIN, Lee Ann and Felicity shared the news of their encounter with Andrew.

"Wow, I can't believe he is ready to tell them everything! Lee Ann, you have become a regular Nancy Drew," Katrina remarked.

"No, she's more like Mariska Hargitay in Special Victims Unit," Jasmine observed. They all laughed at this.

"Will Andrew's story be enough? Do you think the police will bring Samantha in for questioning?" David asked no one in particular.

"Something tells me it isn't enough. Who even knows where Samantha has gotten to and how long it will take for them to find her? We need to confront Samantha with her crime," Lee Ann announced.

"But baby, we don't even know where she is?" David moaned.

"Hmmm, well, we know she is probably married because we can't find any record of her current whereabouts using her old name," Katrina bemoaned.

"I wonder if maybe we should check to see if Samantha hooked up with someone in their friend group or maybe even Andrew's best friend. It could have been a way of getting back at Andrew for dumping her," Jasmine speculated.

"Hey, that's not bad logic, Jasmine," Lee Ann agreed. She went outside and called Andrew to ask him about this possibility. He told her that he did indeed have a best friend that went to Farthington at that time. He had lost touch with him after school and had no idea if he had gotten married to Samantha or anyone else for that matter, though he didn't rule out the possibility. He told her that his best friend's name was Harold Campbell.

A quick internet search brought the group what they were looking for. Sure enough, there was a Samantha Campbell married to a Harold Campbell, living in Franklin, TN about sixty miles from Farthington. A plan was quickly hatched to confront her and see if there was any way they could convince her to come forward about what she'd done. The group had only three days before classes resumed, and other students were already beginning to return to the dorms. Charles had left a day earlier, needing to get back to his business, and David had to leave in two days when he was due back at work. Lee Ann could feel the impending sense that they needed to act right away to protect the students from an unhinged Cassie. They were unable to find a phone number, but they did have the address.

"Well, there's no time to lose. We need to make the drive up to Franklin in the morning," Lee Ann stated.

"I'm definitely coming this time," David insisted. "It's one thing to contact someone who was a witness, but you're confronting the person who actually did the deed; it may not be pretty."

"No, you're right, but we can hope there may be some willingness on her part to come forward after living with such terrible secrets for so long. She will unburden herself greatly with a confession," Felicity mused.

"Jasmine and Katrina, I want you guys to hold down the fort and report back to us if anything weird happens while we're gone. I'm sure Samantha will already be intimidated enough with three people confronting her. Plus, it may not be safe," Lee Ann insisted.

"So, what do you mean by weird? What can we expect to have happen?" Katrina asked. She and Jasmine looked at each other with more than a hint of trepidation.

"Hopefully nothing, but Cassie is still out there, and we have to do what we can to prevent anyone from getting hurt," Lee Ann answered.

"I have a hunch that she won't interfere with our efforts or anyone who may be trying to bring everything into the light. That is what she needs," Felicity pointed out.

"Ok, good. That sounds much better," Katrina said, taking a deep breath. Lee Ann laughed as Katrina walked quickly past one of the windows, not wanting to look out into the night as she made her way to the kitchen to get a glass of water.

Later that night, after the group dispersed to go to their hotel rooms, Lee Ann received a call from Charles.

"Hey dad, what's up?"

"Hey punkin. You doing ok?" he asked, sounding a bit more concerned than usual.

"Fine dad. We're going over to Franklin tomorrow to confront Samantha," she shared.

"I don't know, hun. We're talking about confronting someone who allegedly committed murder. She may not take too kindly to the accusation or her loved ones for that matter. I think it's time to go to the police."

"The problem is we don't have any evidence. All we have is Andrew's account, which is a lot, but it's not enough. We need her confession or some evidence, and as far as I know there is no evidence," Lee Ann went on.

"Ok, punkin, I know I can't stop you when you have your mind set on something. Just promise that you'll take the greatest care and be sure to take David with you," Charles insisted.

"Don't worry, I wouldn't be able to convince him to stay behind even if I wanted him to."

"Sorry I can't be there for you. Like I said before, I blame myself for what you're going through. If only I hadn't been so pigheaded and insisted on you going there...."

"Dad, we've already been through this. Don't do this to yourself. I don't blame you anymore," she said.

"That means so much to me. We'll all be hoping and praying that dragging the truth into the light can bring an end to all of this. After this is over, if you want to go to art school, I'm open to have conversations about it."

"Thanks dad. We'll cross that bridge when we come to it. Meanwhile we have an angry spirit to appease," Lee Ann sighed.

"I know I say it a lot, just be careful punkin," Charles implored.

"Ok, ok, dad. I'm glad to hear you call me punkin again by the way."

"Don't mention it..." Just then, Lee Ann had another call coming in. It was Andrew.

"Hi Lee Ann, it's Andrew. I just wanted to call and say that if you are going to confront Samantha, I want to be there. I may be able to help you convince her," he said.

"Sure! That would be great," she responded, feeling reassured by this.

CHAPTER
TWENTY-ONE
CONFRONTATION

Harold Campbell straightened his tie and prepared to leave the house now that his lunch break was over. His real estate business was only a few short blocks away, and he often walked home for lunch. Samantha paced about the floor in the kitchen, trying to come up with things to do to occupy her mind. Harold was growing increasingly worried about her and wanted her to receive more help than her usual weekly therapy session.

Harold started as his wife dropped a dish onto the kitchen floor, shattering it into pieces.

"Are you ok?" he asked, rushing into the kitchen to help her pick up the shards.

"I'm fine. Just fine.." Samantha was breathing faster than normal as if she were catching her breath the way children do between sobs.

"No, you're not. We've got to get some help; more than just Dr. Phillips."

"I like Dr. Phillips," Samantha responded.

"That's fine, but it's obviously not enough."

"Harold, I just want to be free of this; and I feel like I never will unless... unless..I.."

"Confess? And spend the rest of your life in jail for something that happened so long ago?"

"It doesn't matter how long ago it was. I can't live with this..." Samantha's gasps were now coupled with tears.

"I won't let you.." Harold said as he came up and grabbed her hand softly. He pulled her up from where she was hovered over the broken glass and held her tightly.

Lee Ann, Felicity, and David pulled up in Felicity's car in front of a stately white house with three columns lining the front porch.

"Well, this is the place," David stated as his phone announced that they had arrived at their destination. Andrew had arrived a moment earlier and was waiting for them in his car. They all got out and assembled in the driveway.

"So much for having a small group for this," Lee Ann stated.

"In this case it may be good to have safety in numbers," David said.

"Samantha is not likely to try anything rash. The worst that will probably happen is that they will insist that we leave which I would say is likely," Andrew shared.

Harold and Samantha heard the cars pull up. Harold went to the front room and peaked out of the curtain. He watched as Lee Ann, Felicity, David, and Andrew approached the front door.

"What the?" Harold stated

"Who is it?" Samantha asked as she entered the front room.

"It's.... it's Andrew, and he has two women and another man with him. I don't recognize them."

"Andrew?" Samantha could feel the guilt rising in her chest forming a blockage that made it difficult for her to breathe. She sounded as if she might hyperventilate.

'Honey, breathe!" Harold said as he put his arms around her.

Just then, the doorbell rang.

"What do they want?" she asked.

"I don't know, but I'll take care of it!' Harold declared. His hands were shaking as he turned the knob to open the door.

They agreed that Andrew would initiate the conversation as the couple were already familiar with him.

"Harold, we need to talk to Samantha," Andrew stated, getting right to the point.

"We have nothing to talk about. We are not interested in dredging up the past!" Harold tried to shut the door, but Andrew stuck his foot out and blocked him.

"This is not going to end until we do the right thing!" Andrew's voice rose in volume, soaked with urgency.

"Let them in," Samantha calmly asked.

"Are you sure?" he responded, turning to her.

"Yes, Andrew's right."

"Ok, Andrew," Harold answered, opening the door.

"We're sorry to show up this way, but we couldn't find a phone number," Felicity stated.

"And you are?" Harold inquired.

"I'm Felicity, a friend of Lee Ann's here who has had some encounters with Cassie. She is not at rest."

Harold and Samantha looked at one another in astonishment as Lee Ann recounted the situation from her arrival at Farthington up until recent events.

"I knew that she was back. I've been having dreams, the worst dreams you could ever imagine," Samantha confessed.

"I'm having them too," Andrew stated.

Lee Ann looked at Samantha who was quivering and sobbing softly. She felt a most profound pity for her in that moment that she hadn't expected. In fact, everything about her was the opposite of what she expected, which was defiance and denial. She could see that Samantha was not a cold-hearted beast the way she had built her up in her mind.

"So, what is it you want to do about this exactly?" Harold questioned, revealing more than a hint of impatience in his tone.

"There is only one thing to do and that is to confess. We must go right now to the police and tell them everything that happened on that awful night!" Andrew insisted.

"NO!" Harold exclaimed. It shocked Andrew to hear him this way as he was used to a more mild-mannered nature although he hadn't seen his friend in quite some time. Harold stepped in front of Samantha as if to put a barrier between his wife and the others. His fists were clenched as if he were prepared to fight Andrew.

"Yes, he's right," Samantha declared. "I'm ready." She put her hand on her husband's shoulder and took a deep breath.

"No, honey, no!" He turned to hug her, unable to hold back the tears.

"It's ok. I feel better just knowing I can lift this burden," she answered.

For several moments, they all stood there in silence as the heaviness of the moment settled upon all of them. Lee Ann felt a tear creeping from the corner of her eye as her empath tendencies took over.

An hour later, Samantha turned herself into the sheriff's office after sharing the entire story, including the attempted cover-up. The officers present were shocked to see her standing before them making confessions about an incident they had only heard about from a decade long past.

Back at the dorm, the entire group of friends were quiet and pensive as they absorbed the gravity of the situation.

"So, is Cassie satiated now?" Katrina blurted out, always being the one to speak out loud the words that everyone was thinking.

Lee Ann and Felicity looked at one another. Felicity closed her eyes as she gripped Lee Ann's hand as Lee Ann did the same. Lee Ann shook her head.

"She's not quite ready. There's one more thing...." Lee Ann responded.

Later that night, Headmaster Blevins was tossing and turning again, unable to get to sleep. He had been this way for a couple of months, and it had begun to take its toll on him. He had thought about taking time off, but it wouldn't do for him not to be present during the start of the semester. His eyes, which were normally deep-set, now seemed to have grown into cavernous tunnels. His hands trembled and his armpits pooled with sweat as he gripped his pillow. A patch of moonlight moved across his face, causing him to gaze out of the window, which he normally did his best to avoid, fearing the presence of Cassie. As quickly as the moonlight flashed across his face, it was obscured by something blocking it. He tucked his head back under the pillow, knowing who or what it probably was. A wind whipped up outside blowing with an unnatural force against the walls of the dwelling.

"Time to pay......." A hushed voice spoke on the wind. Headmaster Blevins couldn't take any more. He threw the covers off his body and got to his feet, keeping his eyes fixed on the window. He fully expected to see Cassie's hideous expression leering at him, but instead, the light of dawn began to slowly take over the space occupied by the inky darkness. Headmaster Blevins took a deep breath, feeling relieved by its presence.

"Thank God for the dawn!" He said aloud as he continued to watch the light filter in.

Something else caught his eye as he continued to look out of the window. A group of students had begun to gather in the main quad, which was now visible to him in the growing light. This was very unusual as there weren't normally so many students on campus a week out from the start of classes. They all seemed to be looking down at something amid the crowd. Headmaster Blevins quickly threw on some clothes, feeling the compulsion to see what the fuss was all about.

He ran out to the group, some of which turned to look at him.

"What's the meaning of this? What are all of you standing around gawking at?" he asked. The students seemed puzzled by his irritated tone. They parted to allow him to walk into the middle of the group and see the object of their curiosity.

"No, it couldn't be! I destroyed it!" he called out. The students watched him, most of which were quiet but a few whispered amongst themselves. Headmaster Blevins walked up and picked up the object of his disdain. It was that dreaded diary of Samantha's with its mocking flowery, colorful cover. As he thumbed through the pages, he was astonished to find that none of the pages were ripped out and there were no burn marks on it as there should have been.

"How can this be? NOOOOO!" he yelled out as the astonished students continued to look on in stunned silence.

The headmaster woke himself from the dream when he cried out. He sat up in bed, realizing that the light that he thought was the sun was the illumination of the moon which captured him as if he were standing in a spotlight. Before him a shadowy figure stood perfectly still. A feeling of dread and terror crept over the headmaster as he realized that he was wide awake, alone with Cassie.

"The truth is coming to light. They are coming Headmaster Blevins!" Cassie hissed as she moved close enough for the moonlight to reveal her features. Her face revealed an expression of satisfaction, almost peace. There was a rosiness where once there was a sickly, greenish tint to her translucent complexion.

"NO, NO!!!!" he shouted as he lunged at her from his bed. He fell to the floor as her image dissipated. Outside, he could hear a car pulling up. He threw on his clothes and began to frantically throw items into an overnight bag.

"Mr. Blevins, open the door!" A commanding male voice demanded.

Headmaster Blevins swallowed hard, threw his bag over his shoulder, and exited through the back door. Unfortunately for him, there were men in dark suits waiting for him there.

"Mr. Blevins, you must come with us," one of them spoke, flashing a badge in the process. The headmaster uttered a series of whimpers and sobs as he was carried off with his hands cuffed behind his back. They led him to a black SUV that waited outside his living quarters. The few students and staff that were on campus looked on in astonishment as the light of dawn illuminated the proceedings.

Lee Ann sat straight up in bed, feeling the warmth of the sun on her face. She looked out at the perfect day that was shaping up to be clear and free of clouds. The peace and calm that she felt eased her mind and was paired with the sudden realization that Cassie was finally ready to move on. Lee Ann immediately took her phone and sent a group text to everyone.

It's over, I can feel that Cassie is finally at peace. She is ready

CHAPTER
TWENTY-TWO
RESOLUTION

The group of friends assembled at Lee Ann's cabin on the last day before classes were due to begin. They waited until the sun sank low to make their way to the top of Whispering Falls, a time when they knew they'd be most likely to contact her. Lee Ann, David, and Felicity led the group followed by Jasmine and Katrina. Once they came to the open space just above the falls, Lee Ann stopped and turned towards David.

"Wait here while Felicity and I go to her," she instructed them. David and the others nodded.

"Don't worry, this is close as I'd like to get," Katrina joked.

"Yeah, I'm good right here," Jasmine echoed.

"If you need me, I'll be right here," David reassured her.

"I know," Lee Ann answered with a smile.

Lee Ann and Felicity stopped about three feet from the cliff's edge listening to the quiet chatter of the waterfall. The volume of water had lessened due to the lack of rain in recent days.

"Are you here, Cassie? It's Lee Ann," Lee Ann spoke out. She and Felicity looked around them, feeling something not unlike a charge in the air such as one might feel just before a lightning strike.

"Yes," a voice reverberated from an area of space near the edge of the falls. The quality of her voice had changed. It didn't sound as anguished and aggressive and had lost its guttural quality.

"I'm here!" Cassie spoke as her translucent figure materialized. Her expression was peaceful, and her eyes were no longer aglow with a spiteful red glare.

"But not much longer, thanks to you," she said as she and Lee Ann smiled at one another.

"I did what I could. I'm just sorry that you had to remain here for as long as you did."

"It's like a dream, but one that's lasted the length of all these years. It's hard to explain because time is different now. It's like it's been one long night since it all happened. I was unable to move on even though deep down I knew I was supposed to, somehow. My thoughts would return to what had happened to me and I could think of nothing other than bringing those responsible to justice. Now that that's done, I realize that that's what I was holding onto, the injustice of it all. It kept me here and kept me trapped in an angry state. Everything changed when you came, Lee Ann. I know it sounds crazy."

"Not to me, this isn't my first rodeo," Lee Ann said.

"I could feel your presence here and I was drawn to it. It's like a light that shown out and called to me. I know it sounds weird."

"No, actually it doesn't sound weird at all," Lee Ann remarked, sharing a smile with Felicity.

"Someone else is here," Felicity suddenly spoke. Lee Ann looked at the area of space beside Cassie and had the same sensation; an energetic presence that soon materialized into a familiar figure, that of Connor.

"Connor? But how and why?" Lee Ann called out in her confusion.

"Katy," Connor answered.

Lee Ann gasped at this realization feeling both perplexed and dumbfounded that she had never made the connection.

"But how did I not know all this time? Why didn't you tell me?" Lee Ann asked. Katy and Cassie looked at one another, then Katy spoke again,

"I was there to guide you and assist you. I didn't want to scare you, and I'm sorry that I kept my identity a secret. We just felt that this was the best way," Katy shared, her expression was plaintive and compassionate.

"The truth is you were the only friend I had here this whole time," Lee Ann revealed.

"I was happy to be that for you and to help you put all of the pieces together," Katy answered.

"She was my only friend during my time at Farthington as well," Cassie concurred.

"I understand; I'm not upset, although I still think I should have figured out who you were. So much of what happened makes sense now, like the fact that I never saw you except when I was alone," Lee Ann reasoned as Katy nodded.

"What matters now is that you are ready now, both of you," Felicity stated.

"Yes, I'd say we hung around here long enough. It's time to move on. I can't tell you how much lighter I feel, now that I'm no longer holding onto that anger. Strange thing how we can keep ourselves so bound by our feelings. I hope you have come to find that out as well," Cassie stated.

"I have. When I first came to Farthington, I couldn't focus on anything because I was mad as hell at my dad for making me come here. It took a while for me to see that he was only doing what he thought was best for me because he loves me. Now he can see how his decision affected me and he's sorry for it. That makes me love him even more than before," Lee Ann shared.

"Yes, they were meant to help you just as you were meant to help them. And your anger helped to draw Cassie to you. She identified with it," Felicity reasoned.

Cassie nodded in response for she knew it to be true.

"Now it's time for us to go, but I just want to thank you for everything you've done, Lee Ann. You're one of us. You know, one of those girls that don't quite fit in, but has that something the others don't have but wish they did," Cassie said.

"Yes, and thanks for being a great friend," Katy agreed.

"Yes, now be at peace and maybe I will see you again when the time is right," Lee Ann shared.

"Until then," Cassie and Katy said together as they turned away, looking out towards the cliff's edge.

"Until then," Lee Ann answered.

Cassie and Katy looked at each other, joined hands and took a step off the edge of the cliff just beside the tumbling waters. As they did, their images scattered into beams of light that danced and became one with the spray, dancing endlessly against the rocks and were gone.

"It's done," Lee Ann called out, turning towards her friends who waited beside the clearing.

The group walked quietly back down the trail, each of them lost in their own thoughts. Lee Ann thought of Connor again, shaking her head again for not realizing who or what she was.

"Why didn't I realize that Connor wasn't flesh and blood?" she finally asked Felicity who was walking in front of her.

"She was meant to have her role, and you weren't meant to realize it. She helped you the same way that she helped Cassie. In fact, it seems that she fell into a loop of behavior similar to what she experienced just before her own death."

"You mean, I was a part of her loop, but how?"

"As I said before, Cassie had attached herself to you, she both identified with you and was fed by your energy. You were actually in a struggle to maintain your own identify and not be subsumed by Cassie's energy. Connor, I mean, Katy identified with you the same way she identified with Cassie when she was alive. You were her best friend, and she was yours. I know it's confusing and strange."

"No, I understand what you're saying. It all makes sense now," Lee Ann responded.

"Well, I'm glad it makes sense to you because I'm totally confused," David admitted from just behind Lee Ann. They all laughed together just as they reached the trailhead. The light of day suddenly shone down on them as they emerged from the forest.

Everyone respected what Lee Ann had been through, so no one asked her questions about what had taken place although they each had some that could be addressed when she was less physically and emotionally spent. They returned to Lee Ann's dorm and began to say their goodbyes. David had to be at work the next day. Jasmine was to begin an internship at a law firm in Mt Juliet. Katrina was due to begin studying medicine at Vanderbilt on a full ride scholarship in two days. Felicity didn't have any clients for the remainder of the week, so she didn't feel quite as hurried as the others.

David walked hand in hand with Lee Ann as they made their way to the parking lot.

"Are you going to finish the semester here after everything that's happened?" David asked.

Lee Ann looked all around her at the beautiful scenery and the sunshine glinting off of the pebbles on the walkways that led from the dorms to the main parking lot.

"You know, I think I'm going to. I know it might seem strange after everything that took place here, but I feel like that's been lifted now. I know for sure that any restless spirits in the vicinity have for sure been dealt with. If I go somewhere new, I might be right where I started again." She and David laughed at this.

"I'm going to miss you so much. I have to admit I was kinda hoping this whole incident might make you want to come home...to Laverne," David admitted.

"Babe, I don't know if I want Laverne to be my forever home. It will always be my hometown and a place I will come home to for visits."

"So, what are you saying exactly?" David was unable to hide the worry on his face.

"Don't worry! I didn't mean that I didn't want to be with you anymore. I will visit home as much as I can, and you can visit me here. I just mean in the future I don't want to live in Laverne. It's way too small and too confining for what I want to do."

"What do you want to do?"

"I want to see the rest of the country and the world. I don't want to live in some narrow little town where everyone knows your business and looks up their nose at you for not thinking the way they do."

"I get that," David answered. Lee Ann turned to look at him and smiled.

"What?" he asked.

"You, you're making progress. Before, you would continue to try and convince me to stay in Laverne. David, we can go together wherever we want, and we still have our whole lives in front of us," Lee Ann reminded him. She knew they had had this discussion several times that this wouldn't be the last.

"I know you're right. I just wish we lived in the same place, that's all," He bemoaned.

"We will, David. We will," she said as she took his hands in hers and looked into his eyes. They kissed and embraced for what felt like an eternity, one that Lee Ann didn't want to let go of. She felt so secure and loved in his arms; she began to sob softly thinking of how difficult it would be to finish the term without him there with her.

"I'll be back as soon as I can come visit," he assured her.

"I know," she said as she stood and watched him drive away. Felicity came walking up behind her, followed by Jasmine and Katrina.

"He will find his way," Felicity stated, sensing Lee Ann's thoughts.

"I'm worried that he won't ever move out of Laverne," she shared.

"It will be hard for him, but he must work through it on his own," Felicity answered.

Lee Ann turned to greet her friends. Their presence always lifted any heavy emotions she was dealing with.

"Thank you both so much for being here for me. You can't realize how invaluable it is for me just to have both of you present for moral support." Jasmine and Katrina beamed as they both hugged Lee Ann.

"Glad to be of service! Just hope the next time we get together, it can be under less, um, weighty circumstances," Katrina remarked.

"I second that. Let's have a girls' weekend somewhere that there aren't any woods or creepy legends and maybe a hot tub," Jasmine stated as they all laughed.

Felicity was the last to leave. She looked long and hard at Lee Ann to gauge her mood. She was worried even though she knew that things would settle down at least for the time being.

"Are you going to be ok? I can stay for another day or two if need me I don't have a client until the end of the week," Felicity allowed.

"I'm fine, just lost in my thoughts. I have definitely learned some things about myself through this last ordeal," Lee Ann shared.

"Oh really? Do tell!"

"Well, I realized that right before I came to Farthington, I was running from myself. I was running from home, from past events, from my abilities. I just wanted to be a normal college student going off to focus on my studies."

"And what did you find?"

"I can't run from myself or what I've been called to do. It will always find me. Or it might be more fitting to say, THEY will always find me," Lee Ann revealed, managing to smile.

"It's not easy being an empath- especially someone with gifts such as yours. I know it's hard but try and look at it as such- a gift that enables you to help others. Allow yourself to feel good about helping Cassie and Katie. Without your presence, they would have continued to wander around, lost and angry and unable to move on," Felicity rubbed Lee Ann's shoulder in a comforting gesture.

"I suppose you're right," Lee Ann acknowledged. They embraced one last time before Felicity turned to leave.

On the way back to the cabin, Lee Ann noticed a familiar group of girls eyeing her from the other side of the parking lot. It was Gina and her friends. They waved to her, motioning for her to come over to where they were standing.

"Hey," Lee Ann said as she searched the faces of her former enemies. Becky, Gina, and Claire all had expressions that seemed solemn, friendly, and sympathetic all at once.

"How are you doin'?" Gina asked.

"I'm holding up ok. I guess all of you heard about Headmaster Blevins?"

"I just can't believe the lengths that they went to cover up what happened to those poor girls," Becky acknowledged.

"My parents want me to leave the school after this term," Claire revealed.

"Really?" Lee Ann asked.

"Yeah, the reputation of this school is sure to suffer now that the news is out about the scandal. Still, I don't want to leave," Claire admitted.

"I'm stayin'. I've got a full ride and it's going to take more than a couple of ghosts and a scandal to get rid of me," Becky declared as they all laughed.

"How about you, Lee Ann?" Gina asked.

"Hmmm, well, I'm definitely finishing out the term. Beyond that, who can say?" Lee Ann stated.

"Well, we would like for you to hang out with us sometime real soon. This Friday, we were all thinking about driving up to Nashville for the weekend. We could go in on a hotel room and just make a weekend out of it. Might do us some good to get a little change of scenery," Gina declared. Lee Ann stood there a moment, stunned and flattered. She thought back to high school and how strange it would have felt if Mary Hartford had asked her to hang out like this. She laughed slightly thinking about it.

"What?" Gina asked as a reaction to her laugh.

"Oh nothing. I would be more than honored to go with you!" Lee Ann answered.

"Great! Gina said.

"Well, I need to start getting my stuff unpacked. I only just got back and classes start tomorrow," Claire stated.

"Yeah, me too," Becky echoed.

They three of them waved to Lee Ann as they made their way across the quad. Lee Ann smiled and shook her head thinking about how things had turned around. She turned to gaze back in the direction of her cabin and contemplated the thought of being alone for a while. She was surprised to find that she was pleased with this prospect. It would give her time to think about her art- to come to terms with all that happened and find some way to express that. Ideas began to float around in her head as she made her way back.

TWENTY-THREE

MANIFESTATIONS

M rs. Renford, head of Farthington's Communication and Fine Arts Dept. ran around searching for Lee Ann as she made the last preparations for the end of the year student art exhibition. She was tall with broad shoulders and a curly, dark mop of hair. She wore a tan kimono-like shawl and several yellow and orange necklaces that jangled as she walked. She cleaned off her thick glasses and stopped to look at an abstract painting by Elizabeth Garner, a sophomore who was minoring in art. Elizabeth walked up to gauge her teacher's reaction to her choice for the show.

"Have you seen Lee Ann?" she asked instead.

"Uh, yes she's over there," Elizabeth frowned slightly as she pointed at the refreshments table where Lee Ann was helping Julie arrange the snacks and drinks.

"Great selection, by the way," Mrs. Renford. Elizabeth immediately smiled and gave a small exhale of relief.

David, Jasmine, and Katrina came in together looking around at all of the pieces on the wall. David adjusted his tie nervously. He couldn't remember ever attending an art event before.

"It's ok, man. All you have to do is walk around and look at all the art pieces. They also usually have food at these things too," Katrina said as she lightly punched his arm.

Lee Ann came up to the group with Julie just behind her. She had her hair tied back and wore a flowing, black dress and tall heals. David stood there with his mouth agape for a moment.

"Well hello there," Lee Ann said, closing his mouth with her hand. David became self-conscious and blushed.

"It's just, well, you look so...." David fumbled to find the right words.

"She's hot. Just go on and tell her," Katrina teased as everyone laughed.

"Come over here. I want to show everyone what I've been working so hard on these past few months," Lee Ann motioned for everyone to follow her past the refreshment table to a small nook where she had all of her pieces set up. Mrs. Renford, having finally found Lee Ann, ran up behind her.

"Oh, there you are dear. I Just wanted to see if the refreshment table was ready. You know the new Headmaster, Dr. Mullins is due to arrive any minute and I want to make sure everything is just so," she uttered.

"Yes, Mrs. Renford, it's all ready to go," Lee Ann answered as she turned back to her friends. Felicity walked up just in time to see her explain her work.

"Hey!" Lee Ann hugged Felicity, lighting up what was already a glowing expression of excitement on her face.

"You all should really see what Lee Ann has done with this art dept. Why you could say that there really wasn't one until she came along. Now we have several students signing up for drawing, painting and sculpting classes that barely had anyone in them before. She has really done a lot for us: organizing a fund raiser and this student exhibition, the first of its kind at Farthington," Mrs. Renford bragged as she pushed her dark curls from her shoulders.

"Well, I just wanted someone besides myself to know about how great the Art department classes are," Lee Ann answered. Mr. Stevens taught drawing and painting while Mrs. Renford handled Art History and sculpture. Together they made up the tiny dept. that would soon grow to hire a new teacher thanks to Lee Ann's fundraising efforts.

"You can try and be modest if you like, but I'm really impressed," Jasmine said.

"I second that," echoed Katrina.

David stepped up beside Lee Ann and kissed her on the cheek.

"Me three."

"It's time for everyone else to discover what we've all known all along: Lee Ann is a thoughtful, smart, talented, and rare individual indeed," Felicity added.

Lee Ann was now blushing and beginning to sweat a bit with nervousness. She couldn't remember the last time she'd had this many people showering her with complements and it made her slightly uncomfortable. She shifted the focus back to her work.

"Come this way everyone. I want to show you the pieces I've been working on," Lee Ann proudly admitted. She led them over to the far corner of the exhibition room to a group of sculptures. The first one she showed them was a sculpture of the falls itself made from aluminum and steel. Every cascade had been painstakingly recreated.

"Whoa, this really does look like the falls," Katrina remarked.

"Stand just here," Lee Ann suggested, moving directly in front of the falls.

"Oh my gosh! There's a figure there, falling," Katrina shared.

"Yes! I had some help from the Physics dept. with that one- it's a hologram and you can only see it if you stand in just the right place," Lee Ann said.

"Wow, I see it!" David stated, taking Katrina's spot.

Jasmine was looking at a portrait that Lee Ann did an oil painting of Connor sitting in her bunk bed with her legs dangling over like she always used to do. She painted it completely from memory and the colors were bold and impressionistic.

"I feel like she is really looking into my soul!" Jasmine stated.

There was also a self-portrait that Lee Ann had done of herself with a collage of people and things in the background including David and her friends on one side and shadowy figures on the other. I was meant to illustrate the conflict that she'd experienced as of late between trying to maintain normalcy and the instinctual compunction to embrace her gifts and the souls seeking her aid.

Lee Ann's personal favorite was a life-sized sculpture of Cassie. She stood boldly with her arms crossed in the familiar black t-shirt and ripped skirt and tights looking much like she did the last time Lee Ann saw her before the light took her. Lee Ann wanted to make it a point to depict Cassie as a strong young woman, not a monster that terrorized the girls of the dorms.

"She really looks like a badass," David whispered in Lee Ann's ear.

"She was. I want everyone to see her the way she was in life," Lee Ann answered.

"You did an amazing job. I have to say, this is one of the most impressive student arts shows I've ever attended," Felicity remarked.

"I have to agree," Shirley said after sipping her champagne.

"You should have seen Lee Ann growing up; she was always drawing in her sketchbook out by the creek or deep in the woods."

"Yep, that's my girl. We've known for years that she's the next Georgia 'O Keefe or somethin'," Charles crowed proudly, naming the only female artist that he could think of at that moment.

Lee Ann began to blush; she wasn't used to being the center of attention although she had to admit to herself that she was rather enjoying it.

As the others moved on from Lee Ann's work to the others, Charles took her aside for a moment.

"Hey hun, how are you feeling about Farthington? I know I've said it already, but I want to apologize again for my insistence on you coming here. I want you to know Shirley and I have been talking and we both agree that you should go to art school if that's really what you want to do," Charles's eyes were watery with sympathy and remorse.

"You know, considering what a hard time I had when I first came here and how angry I was about it, I have really grown to love it. I have resolved everything with the girls who hated me at first, heck I would even consider them to be my friends at this point. I love the campus surrounded by the mountains even despite what happened at the waterfall. After everything was resolved, it ended up being the first place for me to focus on my work. We have really grown the little art dept. here and I want to continue that work. I'm staying," Lee Ann concluded.

"Are you sure that's what you want?" Charles said, putting both of his hands on her shoulders so he could look into her eyes.

"Yes, Dad. Don't worry, I'm no longer upset with you. The anger I was experiencing was part of what attracted Cassie to me and it was very unhealthy.

"You don't know how happy that makes me, Punkin. I'm just so proud of you and all the work you've done. You have really blossomed into an incredible artist and an amazing young lady," Charles proudly stated. Lee Ann blushed and smiled as she hugged him. Shirley wiped a tear from her eye and hugged Lee Ann as well.

"I'm so proud of you too, Lee Ann," Shirley said.

"I can see why you are so proud," an unfamiliar voice spoke up. Everyone in the group focused their attention on the speaker. It was a tall woman with flowing red hair in a business suit wearing retro-style tortoiseshell glasses.

"Allow me to introduce myself. My name is Harriet Klinger with Hollis Gallery."

Lee Ann's mouth fell open; she knew who the woman was and was familiar with the Hollis Gallery which was a well known and respected gallery that only established artists were shown in.

"Hi, yes, I know who you are," Lee Ann replied. Her friends looked on in astonishment and delight.

"I want you to know that I'm very impressed with what I see here today! Your work struck a chord with me. It made me remember what I was like when I first became an artist, the way I would express very personal things in my pieces. I can tell that you have a lot to convey and that you have lived through a lot in your short number of years." Harriet's voice was both comforting and a bit pompous in Lee Ann's opinion, but she was overwhelmed with joy to hear such words come from someone she knew and admired.

"I would in fact be interested in having an exhibition of your work at the Hollis," she suggested almost too casually for Lee Ann to believe.

"What? Are you serious? I mean, thank you! I'm overwhelmed with excitement and gratitude right now. Thank you so much!" Lee Ann responded. Katrina and Jasmine looked at each other, both of their mouths were agape. David stood proudly behind Lee Ann, glowing with pride. Shirley leaned in and whispered in Charles's ear,

"Can you believe it?"

"Our girl is truly amazing," he answered. Shirley smiled ear to ear hearing him call Lee Ann 'our girl.'

"Here's my card. I will be in touch. In the meanwhile, enjoy your night. You really deserve all the praise you get." Harriet handed her a card with *Hollis Gallery* on it in gold lettering. It was the fanciest business card Lee Ann had ever seen.

"Thank you. Thanks again for taking interest in my work," Lee Ann said.

"Oh my god!" Jasmine exclaimed once Harriet was out of earshot.

"You are amazing!" David added.

"A rare talent!" Katrina chimed in.

"This is the most exciting thing that's ever happened!" Lee Ann's eyes filled with tears of joy as everyone moved in for a group hug.

"Congratulations pun kin, you deserve all the praise and this opportunity," Charles said.

"You are blossoming, and it is truly an honor to be friends with such a talented young woman," Felicity added.

"I wouldn't be here without all of you. Truly, without your

support I'm nothing," Lee Ann said as a tear formed in her eye. For a moment, her thoughts were of Cassie, how she didn't have the support that she had and how her life could have amounted to so much had she not been the victim of such a tragedy.

"You ok, baby?" David asked.

"Yeah, I'll be ok. I'm just a bit overwhelmed is all," Lee Ann answered, trying to fight back the tears.

Felicity sensed her feelings and came over to her.

"Ah, the curse of being an empath. Dear, she is at peace thanks to you. She will no longer roam the forest or mourn under the shadow of the waterfall."

"Thank you for reminding me. I just wish she'd had the opportunities she deserved in life. I just wish I knew why things had to be this way," Lee Ann bemoaned.

"I felt the same way when I was younger. I would rage with righteous indignation when I saw injustice. Over time I came to accept that being angry about it did nothing but self-harm. Instead, I began to see each occurrence, even the tragic ones as an opportunity to learn a lesson. It doesn't mean that we don't still try and do everything we can to be helpful or take action where we can. It means that we don't drown in the sorrows of the world with our empathy. We can both feel it and not be overcome by it." Felicity's words always had a soothing effect on Lee Ann. She smiled and slowly came back to the moment- the joy that she was feeling about showing her work and having it regarded and having everyone she cared about there with her to share it.

EPILOGUE

Back in Laverne, Lee Ann sat on the porch swing of her family's house and listened to the buzzing metronome of cicadas in the trees around her, watching the lights of the fireflies dance against black expanse of forest. Lee Ann thought about how the peaceful evening and ending to the semester at Farthington were in complete contrast to all the chaos it had started with. The school was suffering through the worst scandal it had ever gone through. Thirty students had decided to leave after the truth was revealed about Cassie and the cover up that ensued. There was a new headmaster, a friendly woman named Freda Young, the first female to run the college. Lee Ann felt that it was the beginning of a new era and couldn't wait to return for the next semester.

As her gaze focused on the night sky above her, Lee Ann thought of her mother as she often did when she was alone at times like this. She closed her eyes, took a deep breath, opened them again and realized that she was in a familiar place. The stars once again twinkled around her and nothing, but the sheer emptiness of space supported her where she floated. She felt no fear as she looked to her left and saw her mother there beside her smiling and looking just as young and vibrant as Lee Ann could remember her looking in the prime of her life.

"I'm so proud of you, baby," her mother said as Lee Ann's face radiated with joy.

"I miss you so much, mom. No matter how much time passes...."

"Sweetie, you have already fought that battle against grief and fear. You don't have to keep reliving those moments of your life." Her voice was as soothing as a trickling, refreshing stream.

"I know, I know. I just wish I still had you in my life to help me during those times when I felt like I had no one."

"You will always have me with you, and you have so many others. Even when they aren't with you physically, they are still with you," she said, putting her hand on her heart for emphasis.

"You're right as always. I just would get so angry sometimes...."

"That is what you have conquered, and it won't be the last time."

"Is that the lesson? Felicity said that everything carries a lesson with it if we are just open to it."

"Yes, you were honest with yourself, and you stood in your truth. You were enraged for being made to go to Farthington, for not being listened to as you perceived it."

"Yes, but I'm over that now."

"That's why I'm so proud of you, dear. That anger was destructive; it kept you from being productive and it attracted Cassie to you. She recognized and related to your emotions."

"I know, Felicity said the same thing."

"But you saved Cassie, Katie, and yourself."

"I just wish I could have controlled my emotions better. I feel like a spoiled baby," Lee Ann admitted.

"No need to be so hard on yourself and understand too that not all anger is bad. Your feelings are valid, but It's the way that you react to your feelings that you can learn from. For instance, if anger inspires you to make some positive change or fight for a righteous cause, it could do good."

"Yeah, but I just stewed in my juices until I realized it was holding me back."

"Then you let go."

"Yes, I keep having to learn that lesson, about how not to hold onto things."

"It's a lifelong struggle, believe me. I held onto the notion of what your father should have been for years, and it did me no good. All I did was try to change him without realizing that it just wasn't going to work.

"It wasn't your fault, though. He was the one that screwed everything up..."

"There's that anger again...."

"No, it's ok mom. I had the same notion as you, and I truly did let go of my anger towards him, not that he doesn't still piss me off every now and then." This prompted a laugh from her mother.

"I realized that I was letting my anger shut out the qualities that I do appreciate about him and that I was failing to recognize that he was really trying to be better, trying to cut down on the drinking and be honest with himself and others."

"Yes, we all have our struggles and Charles is facing his own. It does my heart great good to see that and to know how happy he is with Shirley."

"Mom, can I ask you something? Do have you think Cassie and Connor, I mean, Katie would have been doomed to be in that same situation forever if I hadn't intervened?"

"Quite possibly and quite likely. You see, sometimes people or lost souls don't know what they should do or what the right course of action is until the right person opens that door in their minds and helps them to see things differently. Not everyone has the gift that you possess, not only of being more perceptive to the spirit world but being more open to the needs of others. That is a rare gift. You are a rare gift!"

Lee Ann smiled, took her mother's hand, and stared at her lovingly. She didn't need to say a word as her gratitude and love came through in her gaze. Lee Ann's eyes closed as she breathed deeply trying to hold onto the moment for as long as possible.

She opened her eyes and welcomed back the familiar sounds of the crickets and cicadas who had kicked up a rousing chorus as whippoorwills called back and forth to each other.

It's good to be home

The calm of the evening washed over her and stilled her longing for her mother.

ABOUT THE AUTHOR

Russ Thompson is a writer, teacher, and a musician who has been writing works of fiction for over ten years. Much of his work has been described as Southern Gothic in nature. His initial inspiration came from legends and ghost stories from the hills and hollows of his home state of Tennessee. He seeks to examine the human condition and the struggles and triumphs of self-realization within the context of the paranormal/horror genre. His first release in 2014, 'Tales from the Rim' was a collection of short stories inspired by true ghost stories with some completely taken from the imagination. In 2020, he released the first book in a young adult series called 'The Loop Breaker: A Beacon and the Darkness' which tells the tale of a young woman named Lee Ann who discovers that she has the power to communicate with and be contacted by spirits who cannot transition to the next plane of existence. Soon, she finds herself embroiled in a mystery that involves her own family heritage. In 2022, Thompson released an illustrated children's book called 'The Owls of Sedgemount' which tells the story of a group of owls who are trying to save what's left of their forest home with the help of a little boy. 2025 will see the release of the second book in the Loop Breaker series, 'Secrets of the Falls.' He has many more projects on the horizon including a collection of short stories, more children's books, and the third book in the Loop Breaker series.

A BEACON AND THE DARKNESS
DISCOVER MORE TITLES FROM WINTERWOLF PRESS

The Loop Breaker: A Beacon and the Darkness

By Russ Thompson

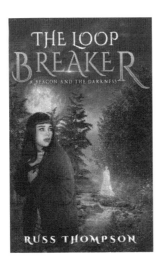

The Loop Breaker: A Beacon and the Darkness is a tale of ghostly mystery and suspense as well as a story of loss and recovery. Sixteen-year-old Lee Ann must face the tragedy of the loss of her mother along with the culture shock of moving in with her father in the tiny town of Laverne.

BETWIXTERS: ONCE UPON A TIME

Fans of Harry Potter, The Goonies, and Percy Jackson will adore

BETWIXTERS: ONCE UPON A TIME

BY LAURA C. CANTU

Magic was a myth to Noah—until a fairy's dying plea drew him into The Dark Wood, where a beast of fangs and shadows stalks him and hungers for his very soul. Noah must decide: attempt a daring rescue and possibly fall prey to the forest's ancient evils or turn his back and watch the fairy—and her magic—fade forever.

SECRET OF SOULS

"A gorgeously imagined new world, filled with action and intrigue. I was enthralled until the very end." **-New York Times Bestseller Lisa Maxwell, author of The Last Magician and UnHooked**

SECRET OF SOULS

BY AUBRIE NIXON

The Empire of Lucent has stood for centuries as a beacon of strength and light. But now an otherworldly realm has unleashed an army of nightmarish creatures upon the peaceful empire, spreading a lethal plague called The Decay which consumes its victims mercilessly from the inside out.

WINTERWOLF PRESS

THANK YOU

We're so grateful you chose to enjoy *Secrets of the Falls*. At Winterwolf Press, our goal is to deliver stories that entertain, inspire, and lift your spirits.

We're more than just publishers—we're like wolves in the wild, bringing together a pack of incredible authors whose stories we believe in. Whether you're a reader hunting for amazing tales or an aspiring author dreaming of joining the pack, we're here to make sure every story finds its way to those who will cherish it.

Thanks for being part of our community.

f facebook.com/winterwolfpress

𝕏 x.com/winterwolfpress

⃝ instagram.com/winterwolfpress

Made in the USA
Columbia, SC
31 October 2024

45373704R00117